MARVELLOUS MARY BROWN AND THE MYSTERIOUS INVITATION

Six guests are invited to the funeral of a man
they don't know. Why are they there?

BERNICE BLOOM

Prologue

FROM BEDDOWS AND PLUNKETT SOLICITORS

DEAR MS BROWN,

WE ARE SAD TO ANNOUNCE THE DEATH OF REGINALD CHARTERS.

HIS FUNERAL WILL BE HELD AT GOWER CHAPEL NEXT TO GOWER Farm Hotel, Llanelli.

IN ACCORDANCE WITH THE DECEASED'S WISHES, WE REQUEST that you arrive on Wednesday by 3pm, prior to the funeral on Thursday morning. You will be free to leave from 3pm on Thursday.

. . .

ALL YOUR EXPENSES WILL BE PAID, YOU WILL STAY IN THE SMART Gower Farm Hotel and you will be more than adequately compensated for your time.

WE URGE YOU TO ATTEND.

HUW BEDDOWS AND GERAINT PLUNKETT
Directors, Beddows and Plunkett Solicitors

Chapter 1

2018

"Hi, Mum, it's me," I said, as I plonked myself inelegantly on the edge of the squashy sofa, and listened for my mother's dulcet tones to come down the phone line.

But there was nothing.

"I heard the news. Are you OK, mum?"

"The news? What do you mean? I'm fine, except for this damn phone. Your father keeps forgetting to charge it."

"I suppose he's distracted, with the bad news about Reginald. He's not too upset, is he?"

"Reginald? What bad news?"

"Mum, he died. I got an invitation to his funeral."

"Your father's godfather?" said mum. She was clearly still having problems with the phone the way she was shouting into it.

"Yes."

"He died?"

"Well, I imagine so. It would be a bit odd to get an invitation to his funeral if he hadn't."

"Oh dear. Oh, that's sad. He'd come out of hospital and was feeling much better. How did he die?"

"I don't know, Mum, that's kind of why I was ringing you…you tend to know this sort of thing."

"I didn't even know he'd died. Oh, that's very sad. Let me call Rosalyn and check. That's really thrown me. How awful. I'll call you right back."

I put the kettle on and read the funeral card again. Definitely Reginald and unquestionably an invitation to his funeral. The service was to be held in a village in South Wales. But, why on earth was I invited? I hardly knew the guy. And why in Wales? And why did I have to turn up at 3pm the day before? So many questions.

The phone rang as I poured my tea and I wedged my mobile between my neck and ear as I added milk.

"Reggie's not dead," said Mum. Her tone was a touch accusatory. "I gave Ros a hell of a shock just now, suggesting that he was. She rushed up to check on him to find him sitting up in bed reading *The Telegraph*, feeling better than he has for years. Why did you say he was dead?"

"I was invited to his funeral, that's why I thought he was dead. It's not an unreasonable assumption. Hang on."

This was crazy. I picked up the card and read it to Mum.

"Reginald Charters?" she said. "I thought you were talking about Reginald Oates."

"Oh." Now I was more confused than ever. "I don't know. I saw Reginald and thought it was him. I don't know any other Reginalds."

"Well, sweetheart, it's not our Reginald."

"This is so odd, mum. It's addressed to me personally, and they have my address and everything. But – I swear – I have no idea who this guy is."

"You must know him from somewhere or you wouldn't be invited to his funeral."

"I don't know him. I've never heard the name before."

"Well then, why have you been invited to his funeral?"

"Good question, Mum," I said. "I haven't got the faintest clue."

AN HOUR LATER I ARRIVED AT MUM'S FRONT DOOR clutching my laptop, a notebook and the invitation that had caused such consternation. I'd been googling the name 'Reginald Charters' for the last hour to no avail. I couldn't find any possible link to anyone of that name. In fact, there were very few Reginald Charters listed on the internet. There was someone mentioned in a big tome all about the modern media, a man listed in a marriage registry in Canada three years ago, and some World War One pilot who couldn't possibly be my Reginald because if he'd fought in the First World War, he'd have to be about 122 years old by now.

Mum and Dad were in the sitting room, looking as confused as I was feeling.

"You must know this man," said Mum. "Perhaps you met him when you went on that safari trip? Or on the cruise? What about that old man you met on the cruise who was travelling abroad to say farewell to his old comrades who'd died in battle. Could it be someone related to him?"

"I don't see how," I said. "I met Frank on the cruise and got to know him quite well but he died soon after we got back.

I never got to know any of his friends or family or anything. Why would any of them invite me to a funeral?"

Dad shook his head and went back to watching repeats of *Morse*, while Mum and I set ourselves up in the back room – laptop open, phones out and books spread across the table. It was like we were running a murder investigation.

"What about the yoga weekend you went on?"

"Nope. I met a yogi, banged my head, lay there as some bloke's tackle fell out of his shorts when he was coming down from downward dog, then came home again."

"Was the yogi called Reginald?"

"Nope."

"What about the bloke with the runaway testicles?"

"Nope."

Mum and I sat there looking at one another, discombobulated and unsure what to do, when my phone rang. It was Ted, my long-suffering boyfriend. "I better take this," I said to Mum. "I haven't seen much of Ted recently; he gets funny with me when I don't take his calls."

I was hoping this would be a cue for Mum to leave the room and let me talk to Ted in peace. I thought she might go and, you know, make me a lovely cup of tea or something. But – no. She sat there looking at me, so instead of exchanging words of endearment with my beloved, I told him about the mysterious invitation.

"Read it out to me," he said.

I read it and waited for his verdict.

"Have you rung the solicitors who sent it?" he asked.

"Oh, no. I haven't. Do you think I should?"

"Er…yes," he said, a little patronisingly. "I'd have thought that would be the first thing you'd do."

I looked at the table in front of me, set up like a major incident room and thought – yes, he was probably right, that should have been the first thing we did, though that wouldn't have been as much fun as going full-scale detective with Mum.

"I'll call them now, and let you know what they say."

I ended the call and told Mum what Ted had suggested.

"OK, you do that while I put the kettle on."

I rang the number on the letter and a soft Welsh accent drifted down the line.

"Beddows and Plunkett Solicitors, how can I help you?" she said.

I went through a rather wordy explanation of the invitation and my confusion.

"I understand," she said. "Let me put you through."

Next to answer the phone was Huw Beddows, one of the partners in the firm. My ridiculous enquiry had sent my call straight to the top.

"I'm sorry to trouble you," I started. "It's just that I've received an invitation to a funeral and I don't believe I know the guy who's died. I wondered whether you could help?"

"I certainly can, Ms Brown," he said.

How did he know my name? I hadn't given it to the receptionist.

I could hear Mr Beddows shuffling papers around on his desk before coming back on the line.

"OK," he said. "Well, I can tell you that Mr Charters specifically asked, on his deathbed, for you to be at his funeral."

"What?"

"Yes, it was his dying wish."

"But – I don't know this guy. How can he want me at his funeral?"

"I didn't know Mr Charters personally but he made it clear

in correspondence, which he put together from his hospital bed, that he was very keen for you to be there. He only invited six people and you are one of them. We will send you a first-class train ticket and can pay for you to stay the night before the funeral. We will pay for all incidental expenses associated with travel and subsistence. We also request and advise that you come to the will reading the morning after the funeral."

"The will?"

"Yes."

"I have been left something in his will?"

As I said that, Mum re-entered the room, teacups shaking on the saucers she was carrying, as she stared at me wide-eyed.

"Yes, I believe you have been left something but I'm not at liberty to discuss any of the contents of the will until it's read formally."

"OK," I replied.

"All the information will be sent to you, Ms Brown, along with tickets and a generous expenses allowance, taxis will be booked to take you to the accommodation and you will be compensated for any loss of earnings."

"Right," I said. "It still seems odd though. And can I just ask you something?"

"Of course."

"How did you know I was Mary Brown? I didn't give my name to the receptionist."

"Because you were the only one who hadn't rung."

"Sorry?"

"The other five people who are coming to the funeral have already phoned up."

"Oh, OK. What did they phone up for?"

"To ask about Reginald Charters, to say they didn't know

who he was and to ask why they had been invited to the funeral."

"What? Really? No one going to this funeral has a clue who the deceased is?"

"That appears to be the case, Ms Brown."

"And you can't tell me any more about Reginald Charters?"

"I don't know anything about Reginald Charters," said Mr Beddows. "I never met him. I was instructed by a private detective who liaised with Mr Charters as he was dying. They have given me envelopes to hand out and strict instructions to follow but other than that I know nothing. I'm as much in the dark as you are. To be honest, I've never known anything like this in my life before."

Chapter 2

THE NEXT MORNING MY TICKETS ARRIVED ALONG WITH AN envelope with £200 in it for "incidental expenses". There were notes and maps containing details of the journey I was to take. Everything had been planned in extraordinary detail: "Come out of the station, a taxi will pick you up there, next to Joe's Ice Cream Parlour which is next to the solicitors' office."

I honestly don't think the government's Cobra meetings are as well organised as this.

Ted had stayed the night so we flicked through the contents of the stiff, brown envelope together.

"Are you going to war, or going to a funeral?" asked Ted, when he saw the detailed maps and notes. There was something quite unnerving about the formality of it all. If it weren't for the bonus £200 tucked inside, I'd have been quite weirded-out by it all.

"What do you think?" I said to Ted.

Ted was silent as he took it in. "To be honest, I'm not at all comfortable. They've given you every detail in the world about how to get there but told you nothing about why you're going. Doesn't that strike you as odd?

"Are you sure it's a proper solicitors' firm? I don't see how it makes any sense to go to some remote place to attend a funeral of someone you've never heard of. And I certainly don't think you should be taking the £200 from them, you don't know what they'll want in return."

"It's for expenses," I said.

"What expenses? Everything you could possibly need is in the envelope."

"Snacks and things, I guess."

"No one could eat £200 worth of snacks on a British Rail journey."

"Is that a challenge?" I asked, but Ted wasn't in the mood for talk of a food challenge. He raised his eyebrows as if to suggest that I wasn't taking this whole thing anywhere near seriously enough.

"When I rang them, it seemed like it was a proper company," I said. "I mean, there was a secretary and she put me through to the partner of the law firm."

"That could have been two nutters sitting in a flat in Birmingham," said Ted. "I just think it's weird." Ted flicked through the notes in front of him. "I'm going to ring them now and see what's going on."

"They're not going to be open yet, are they? It's only half past eight. I doubt there will be anyone there til nine."

"Well, I'll ring at nine then. I want to talk to them. You can't go gallivanting off without us being really sure this is all legitimate." He looked at the tickets again. "You're supposed to be leaving the day after tomorrow. I can't let you go off to some remote village in some part of Wales I've never heard of with a bunch of people we don't know because of some weird dead bloke you've never heard of."

"Well, yes, when you put it like that, I guess it is a bit odd."

"A bit? It's insane. Can you get a couple of hours off work this morning, so we can try and find out a bit more about this?"

Getting time off work can be really difficult because I work in a DIY and gardening centre, and if I'm not in, someone else has to work for me, but I knew Ted was right.

"I'll message Keith and see what he says." I sent a text through to my boss to let him know that a relative had died (I couldn't say "someone I don't know has died"), and explained that I had to go to the funeral and I really needed to sort a few things out first. To my amazement, he came straight back to say he was sorry to hear about my loss and of course it was OK to come in late.

"Now I'm more worried than ever," I said to Ted. "Why is Keith being nice to me? This is all so damn odd. Mad mysterious invitations to funerals and a friendly boss – it's all bonkers."

"Just go and have a shower, get dressed, come back down here and we're going to talk to the solicitors' firm as soon as it opens," said Ted. He was getting all assertive and controlling, it wasn't a side of him I was used to seeing.

"Whatever you say." I gave him a salute before running through to my bedroom to shower and change.

I RETURNED HALF AN HOUR LATER – FRAGRANT AND CLOTHED.

"Have you seen this?" Ted asked, pushing a letter across the table to me. "It was in the envelope."

In scratchy, old person handwriting, the letter said:

. . .

MY DEAR MARY,

WHAT A SHAME I SHAN'T MEET YOU AT THE FUNERAL, BUT I'M *delighted you can attend. This will be a joyous occasion and you will leave feeling full of happiness…uplifted and rejoicing.*

THIS WILL TURN OUT TO BE A WEEKEND THAT YOU REMEMBER *for the rest of your life,* I GUARANTEE YOU.

REGINALD

"OH. MY. GOD! IT'S A NOTE FROM THE DEAD GUY."

Ted read through the letter too, his brow furrowed in concentration as he scanned the inked lines.

"I'm still not convinced. I need to check this out properly," he said. "Come and sit here."

He indicated the seat next to him and put the phone on the table in front of us, clicking it onto loudspeaker. We leaned over it like the French Resistance and Ted dialled the number.

"I was thinking, while you were in the shower, I should come with you. I think it would be much safer if I was there too."

I was torn by this announcement; on one hand I thought it was rather lovely that he wanted to come and keep me safe, and it would be nice to have company on the journey, but the other part of me was quite looking forward to the solo adventure of going off on this bonkers trip to the funeral of someone I didn't know without having a clue why they wanted me there. It appealed to my sense of madness.

"I'm sure I'll be safe," I said. "If I don't feel safe, I can just leave."

"You'll be in the middle of nowhere with a bunch of people you don't know," he said harshly.

A secretary answered the phone in the solicitors' office and Ted got to work, explaining his concerns. He was put through to Huw Beddows and he repeated his distress at what was being asked of me. I'd never seen him so forceful before. It was quite sexy to watch him, to be honest; he wanted to know exactly what was going on, and said that he would be coming with me.

"It's not really the sort of event where partners will be present," said Huw. "She'll only be gone for a couple of days and it would be much easier for everyone if she came alone. The others will be coming on their own. Nothing to worry about at all, sir."

"That makes me more worried than ever. What sort of nutter insists that people must come alone?"

Ted didn't wait for a response from Mr Beddows.

"So, a guy said on his deathbed that he wants a bunch of people who don't know one other to turn up in the middle of nowhere without giving a clue as to why he wants them there and they must come unaccompanied."

"Yes," said the solicitor. "I know it sounds odd and I don't know why he's invited the people he has; all I can do is assure you that Ms Brown will be safe while she is here. She will be staying at Gower Farm Hotel, which is lovely. You have my word that this is a genuine request from a man on his deathbed who wanted to invite these people, I'm sure everything will be revealed over the course of the 24 hours that she's here, but I understand Mr Charters had deeply personal reasons for wanting them to come."

"If this is some dodgy scheme, I will find you and kill you," said Ted.

There was a silence on the end of the phone.

"Did you hear me?" asked Ted.

"It's not a dodgy scheme. We have been a solicitors' firm in this village for over 100 years, I've been working here since I was a 21-year-old fresh out of university, my father, Llyr Beddows, owned this firm before me. This is an unusual situation, I accept, but there is nothing dodgy about it."

Ted finished the call and googled the solicitors' firm, as I had done the day before, and established that – yes – it had been in the village for over 100 years, and the partners of the firm, and their descendants, had been there for decades.

"It seems legitimate and I'm sure you'll be safe, but do you want to go?" he asked me.

"Obviously I'm intrigued," I replied with honesty. "I'd like to know why I've been invited; I think it's worth me going."

"All right, but you have to call me if there's anything dodgy at all, OK?"

"OK," I reassured him.

"And you have to tell me what all this is about. As soon as you know – call me."

"OK," I said, preparing to leave for work. Ted hadn't done anything this morning that I hadn't already done, and we were none the wiser about why I'd been invited but, somehow, because it had been Ted who'd asked, we both felt that I was safer.

Chapter 3

1943

"CLOSER TOGETHER."

Marco winced as he felt the tip of a gun jab him in the side.

"Move. Closer. NOW!"

There was nowhere to move to. He couldn't get any closer to the guys either side of him. The truck was packed full of soldiers; shoved in like sheep being transported to a slaughter-house. Marco shuffled in his seat, doing his best to move up so he didn't earn the wrath of the British soldiers sent to control and humiliate them. He edged towards Lorenzo, his closest friend – the guy he'd fought alongside in the most dreadful conditions. The guard stared at him, and Marco dropped his head and looked down at his filthy trousers and scuffed boots. Returning the stare would only result in angering the man. He had no desire to anger anyone. Not ever. And especially not now.

The truck trundled on, along roads full of potholes that sent them swaying from side to side, crashing into one another, unable to sleep though weary from fear and physical exhaustion. Marco was desperate for water and something to eat. He hadn't washed properly for what felt like months. He'd been serving in Africa where they had been rationed to a single cup of water for washing. It was nowhere near enough for them to clean themselves properly, and they'd railed against it. Now he'd do anything for that one cup of water. Just a drop of water.

When he'd left his lovely home in Italy to join the army, he'd had no idea how hard it would be. The war films he'd watched as a young boy, and the tales he'd read from soldiers returning from the first World War had given no clue as to how horrific it would be. He'd imagined ration packs and whistling in the showers. He'd not considered days without being able to clean themselves and becoming so hungry that he'd be reduced to eating flesh from camels that had been blown up by landmines. He and Lorenzo had faced daily bombings and attacks. He ought to be glad he'd been captured by British forces rather than being forced to stay there any longer, fighting for his life in scorching, oppressive conditions.

But he wasn't. He didn't feel glad at all.

At least he'd known what awaited him every morning when he woke up in Africa; here he had no clue what would happen from one moment to the next. He had no idea what hovered at the end of this long journey through a rainy, bumpy foreign land. He guessed they'd be worked, and starved, to death.

As the lorry trundled along, he thought of his mother and the way she had clung onto him when he left, the sound of her cries still clear in his mind. The sight of his father's face – tight and so full of pain as he tried valiantly not to let his fears and despair show. He was their only son. When he'd gone to war, it had broken their hearts. He squeezed his eyes closed at the memory. Would they know he'd been taken prisoner? Or would they assume he'd died on a foreign battlefield like so many others? He said his own silent prayer that he would live, if not for himself, for his mum.

Marco kept his eyes shut, trying to think of their lovely house in Naples…how spotless his mother always kept it, all the friends who came round, the great big meals she'd host with enough food for dozens more, and wine flowing freely late into those warm Italian nights.

"Off!" shouted a voice, interrupting his thoughts of home. An unfamiliar man pulled open the doors at the back of the truck. "Off. NOW!" he repeated in an arrogant and aggressive tone that was given more menace by his severe countenance. He embodied everything Marco feared about the British.

Marco joined the others in climbing off the truck and marching into an old hut that did nothing to keep off the cold and rain. They were handed thin blankets and told to sleep on wooden planks lying on the floor. Marco walked over to the place he'd been allocated. He was handed water which he drank in one fierce, grateful gulp, but no food. Then he lay down on the wooden slats, wrapped the blanket around him, took one look up at the nasty-looking armed guards who stood at the door, guns cocked, and he closed his eyes. He would probably be shot in his sleep, he wasn't sure that he'd ever make it back to Italy, but for now he was alive. He needed to focus on that…for now he was alive.

. . .

MORNING CAME ABRUPTLY WITH THE SHRILL BLAST OF A whistle and the sound of angry voices blaring through the room.

"Up, up, up," came the growls, as a gun slammed into his side. Marco jumped to his feet and was told to shower, then handed a uniform to wear – it was wine-coloured with a yellow circle on the back and knees. He didn't know what it represented or where he was going next.

After a cold shower, he and the other Italian prisoners were marched back outside and forced onto a cattle truck. It was 6am, he hadn't eaten for days and felt dizzy with fear and starvation. If they wanted to kill them, they were going the right way about it. Marco sat in the truck as it went down the bumpy lanes. He peered out through the back at gorgeous countryside; the beauty of the place outside providing such a vivid contrast to the scene inside the truck where starving and exhausted soldiers sat in fear for their lives.

Then the truck stopped.

An Italian-speaking soldier stood at the front and addressed them. He explained that they were in a country called Wales and they would be working on farms, helping in whatever way was required of them. They would be dropped off, some in small groups, some on their own, and they would have to work hard "or endure the consequences." They would be collected at the end of the day and taken back to the camp. Then the truck rumbled on, stopping every so often as names were called out and men climbed off and met their new masters – farmers who looked surly and confused by the men being foisted on them.

"Lorenzo Alberto," the soldiers shouted, and Marco's closest friend moved to the back of the truck and jumped out, offering a quick backward glance to Marco as he did.

The truck continued, down the narrowest of lanes. "Marco Stilliano," came the shout. Marco stood up and walked to the back of the truck, clambering out and making his way forward, where the officer with a clipboard ticked him off and reminded him that if he put a foot out of line he would be shot.

"You understand me?" asked the soldier.

Marco nodded.

"I said, do you understand me?"

"Yes, sir," said Marco, looking him in the eye. "I understand you."

Marco walked towards the farmer standing with what he assumed were two farm hands near a sign saying 'Gower Farm'. Neither of them appeared to be remotely pleased to see him. It was no wonder, really, he knew he must look a terrible state. He shook hands with the farmer and walked with him towards the house, being watched as he went by the soldiers on the truck.

"Do you speak English?" asked the farmer.

"I speak some," said Marco. "I will learn more."

"Good, my name's Tom and these are Ken and Keith who work with me on the farm."

"I'm Marco," he said, staggering a little as he shook their hands.

"Are you OK?" asked Tom. "Is something wrong?"

"No, I am fine. I will work hard," said Marco. "I promise to work very hard."

"Have you eaten?" asked Tom. "You look thin. Have you been fed?"

"No," said Marco, "but I will be fine. I can work hard."

"Irene," called Tom, as they reached the farmhouse. A pretty woman came out and approached them. Tom said

something to her in a language that Marco couldn't understand and she looked at him and smiled. It was a kind smile
that reminded him so much of his mother.

"Hello, Marco," she said. "I hope you are well."

"Hello, ma'am," he replied. Then she disappeared from
view.

"Sit here," said Tom, going after her. "Stay with him,
boys."

Keith and Ken sat either side of him on the low stone wall,
then Tom came back out with a flask and something wrapped
in tinfoil. "Eat this first," he said.

"Thank you, thank you," said Marco as he tore open the
foil to see a huge chunk of bread. In the flask there was soup, it
was salty and weak but in that moment it was more delicious
than anything he had ever tasted before. He ate the food in
minutes and looked up at Tom. "Thank you," he said. "I will
work very hard, I promise. You are kind people."

"I'm sure you will," said Tom, then he issued an instruc-
tion to Keith. Marco couldn't understand a word of it.

"We're speaking Welsh," explained Tom. "I've told Keith
to take you to the back field and show you what to do."

Marco felt like a different person now he'd eaten something – stronger and more alive than he had in days, and he
threw himself into working as hard as he could. He'd been
labouring for what felt like a few hours when he heard Tom's
voice, as the farmer approached on his tractor.

"Hey, you can stop now," said Tom. "We don't want to
work you to death. The others are all down at the end of the
field having a lunch break. Come on."

"I can work," said Marco. "You already gave me food
today."

"No, you will have a break for lunch every day and a break

for tea in the afternoon," said Tom. "We might be at war but we're not savages. Come on. Food time."

They sat in a circle and Tom handed out the food prepared by Irene.

"What's it like being at war?" asked Keith. "Is it exciting?"

"No," said Tom. "It's not fair to ask that."

"I don't mind answering," said Marco in a voice barely more than a whisper. "It's not exciting. Very frightening, humbling and overwhelming. It's like nothing I've experienced before. It's quite horrible, but I had to fight for my country."

Marco dropped his head as he spoke.

"I think that's enough war talk," said Tom. "How about you tell Marco something about the history of the farm?"

But Keith was too fascinated to let it go.

"Do you support Mussolini? I mean, it's one thing to fight for your country, quite another to fight for Mussolini. He's an evil bastard."

"Come on, that's not fair," said Tom. But Marco raised his hand.

"No – it is fair. I support Italy. Not Mussolini. I fight for my country, my friends."

Along with many of the prisoners, Marco had a great antipathy to the warmongering policies of Mussolini, and to Fascism in general. He tried to explain this to Keith in his best broken English. Keith and Tom nodded and Marco realised they understood him. He smiled broadly, delighted to be able to communicate with these lovely people who had taken him in. Ken was sitting a little apart from them and hadn't said anything to Marco since he'd arrived. Marco didn't know whether the man just didn't like him, or whether he was shy.

. . .

By the time Marco had been at the farm for a week, he felt like he belonged. He was more and more grateful for the decency and kindness of Tom and his family as the days went by. He still didn't understand everything that Keith said because he spoke so fast, but he was getting there. He was starting to understand the words that Tom used regularly and starting to make sense of his gentle, lilting accent. Tom delivered everything he said slowly, to help Marco understand, and he spoke with real warmth and with great kindness in his eyes.

Ken was the only one who Marco struggled to get along with. He had asked Keith whether there was anything he was doing to upset the slim, rather miserable man who he shred his days with. Keith explained that Ken was shy. He had been in an accident a few years previously when he drove over a body on the narrow farm track coming back late one night. The police discovered later that the body was already dead by the time Ken ran over it so there was no suggestion that Ken had killed anyone, but the whole incident had hit Ken hard, and led to him withdrawing into himself.

By day, Marco would work as hard as he could for Tom, and learn as much English as he could from his hosts, when they weren't speaking Welsh, and at night he'd collapse and sleep soundly.

The accommodation, back at the POW camp, wasn't as bad as he'd first feared. On that first night they'd been forced to sleep on a wooden floor, but when they returned from working on the farms, they found they had been moved to the centre of the prison which was a mass of buildings containing proper beds and with a proper roof.

He'd chat to his friend Lorenzo about their experiences,

and compare notes on the days they had endured. Lorenzo was working for a more aggressive, less friendly farmer than Tom, but a man who was reasonable and fair. He was fed regularly and treated reasonably. That was all that any of them wanted.

Marcus found his life had a pattern to it now, a routine; he was eating properly and exercising relentlessly. Muscles were beginning to form where once he had been skin and bone, and colour returned to his cheeks thanks to being based outside all day. Though he and Tom were from different countries and on different sides in the war that was tearing through Europe, they had found common ground in the simplicity of working the land.

"Lunchtime," said Tom, and Marco laid down his tools, wiped his hands on his uniform and climbed onto the tractor next to his boss, sitting quietly as they drove through the field to where the workers were assembled, having lunch. A big chunk of homemade dread dipped in lard and a sliver of fruit pie sat in the box, waiting for him.

"Please say thank you to Irene," he said. "This is so lovely food. Like my mamma used to make."

They all laughed at his kind words delivered in a strong Italian accent.

"Where are you from, in Italy?" asked Tom.

"Napoli," he replied shyly. "My parents are still there."

"When did you last talk to them? Do they know you are alive and well?"

Marco just shook his head. His parents didn't know where he was. They had no idea whether their only son was dead or alive.

"I have lived here all my life," Tom said, sensing that he had upset the boy. "As you know, I live here with my wife Irene and our son, Tom Junior. You haven't met him yet, but you will."

Marco smiled. "It is nice to have a wife," he said. "To have a family, a son with your name."

"I'm sure you will one day," said Tom. "Once this war is over, you'll have a family too."

"I will have a son called Joe," said Marco, emboldened by the confidences shared by Tom. "He will be called Joe after my grandfather; he lives with my mother and father in Napoli. I have no brothers and sisters, but a lovely life. My father run an ice cream shop. The best ice cream in the whole of Italy. The whole of the world."

"I'm sure your father and grandfather must be very proud of you. You are a hard worker. I like that."

Marco smiled and nodded. He had the warmth of the sun on his skin, food in his belly and gentle conversation. He felt alive again. These people had saved him.

"Thank you," he said. "Thank you for everything."

Chapter 4

1943 Six months later…

"Hey, Marco. Can I have some?" said a cautious little voice. Marco glanced down at the small boy looking up at him as he ate his sandwiches.

"Of course," said Marco, handing the little boy the one remaining sandwich in his small, tin box.

"No, Tom Junior, leave Marco alone." Irene raced up to them. "Let him eat his food, you little monster."

"Hey, it's no problem at all. Of course he can have some," said Marco. He knew how difficult it was to get hold of food of any sort with the rationing that was going on, the least he could do was share the food they had kindly given him.

"There you go," said Marco, lifting Tom Junior onto his lap and watching as the boy's eyes lit up when he bit into the soft bread and tasted the saltiness of the scraps of meat they had saved from the previous day's meal.

"Thank you, you're very kind, but those were for you," said Irene crouching down beside him.

"It's really not a problem," he said, jumping up with Tom Junior safely in his arms, when he realised there was nowhere for her to sit.

"Please – sit here," he said, holding Tom Junior on his hip.

"No, goodness, Marco, you've been working since 6am, you're entitled to have a sit down."

"Please take it, I will not sit down while a lady stands. My father would never forgive me. Please, have my seat."

Irene sat down reluctantly, and smiled up at Marco. He was such a kind man, a real gentleman, well brought up and a joy to have working on the farm. He'd made a huge difference in the six months he'd been there – throwing himself into the work and blending in so well with all the family.

Tom Junior still clung to Marco, so the handsome Italian sat down on the grass in front of Irene, putting her son on his lap while they spoke. He'd become close to the family in the time he'd been working on the farm, and had a particularly close relationship with the young boy who loved to be read to by the Italian soldier.

"Tell me all about your book - the *Call of the Wild*," said Tom Junior.

"Goodness, stop hassling the poor man," said Irene. "First, it's his sandwiches, then it's that damn book again. He needs a break."

"It's not a problem at all," said Marco. "I have it here." He pulled out of his bag a small book with a bright yellow cover and saw the look of delight on Tom Junior's face. The book was a novel that his father had given him when he was a little boy in Italy and he'd kept it close by ever since. The book had been shot at and lost then found again, it had been through battles and been across countries. Now it was one of his most prized possessions.

"Tell me all about the squadron leader," said Tom Junior.

The star of the book was Squadron Leader Reginald Charters – a man who seemed to get himself into the most extraordinary number of adventures. Book after book that Squadron leader would be saving lives, leading his men into battle and saving children from certain death. He was swashbuckling, brave and handsome…and Tom Junior loved to hear the tales. Marco turned the page and prepared to read.

"Before you start, Marco – I've been talking to my husband," said Irene, while Tom Junior devoured the remains of the sandwich, licking every finger one by one to make sure he got every crumb.

"Is everything OK?" said Marco. The way Irene mentioned her husband had him worried. The last thing he wanted to do was upset these hosts who had been so incredibly kind to him.

"Yes, everything is absolutely perfect, Marco. In fact, I would say there is just one thing you could do to make us happy."

"Of course," said Marco, ruffling Tom Junior's hair when he realised the young boy was staring up at him. "You've been so kind to me, of course I'm happy to do anything you want. Would you like me to rebuild the fence down at the bottom field where the sheep got out? I can easily take some of the men down there this afternoon. We can work a longer afternoon than usual and get it finished."

"No, that's exactly the opposite of what I want you to do, Marco. What I would really like is for you to take some time off this afternoon. Tom and I are going to the Mart – the place where we sell sheep. Please have a few hours to yourself.

Use the outhouse near the farmhouse, and have a sleep, or read, whatever you like. But you must stop working these insane hours. OK?"

"I do not need a break," he said, more bluntly than he meant. He hoped they hadn't noticed how tired he was. He had tried hard not to show it, and to work diligently to keep them happy.

"Yes, you do, Marco. I insist you take a break. You said you'd do whatever would make me happy. I am telling you that would make me happy.

"Also, would you please write to your mum and tell her you're OK? I'll stick some paper and an envelope on the dining room table for you. Leave the letter there when you've written it and I'll post it for you."

"Thank you," said Marco. "You have been so kind to me, I want to work hard for you every day. I would feel bad doing nothing."

"You mustn't feel bad. I'd love it if you spent some time relaxing and enjoying yourself, and Tom would too. Now – you better get back to your story before Tom Junior explodes with frustration."

"Of course," said Marco, turning to the first page where the big picture of Squadron Leader Reginald Charters in his fine uniform, sat proudly on the page.

At 3pm, Marco waved off Tom, Irene and Tom Junior, chasing after the truck, loaded with sheep, as it went down the narrow winding road, making faces as Tom Junior squealed with delight.

He walked into the house and sat down at the table. He had no idea what to write to his mum, but he picked up the pen, regardless, and looked down at the lovely writing paper all set out for him. He knew that anything he wrote would have to go through censors, so he couldn't say too much, but he could tell his parents that he was safe, and being well looked after.

By the time he'd finished, he'd written around three pages – telling them all about his role in the war so far, with the horror removed so as not to upset his mother. Along with the sanitised version of his fighting experiences, he told them about the farm and how kind the Gower family had been – teaching all about farming, from tending to the land, to milking the goats and looking after the sheep. He told them that Lorenzo was well too, and he hoped that everyone at home was smiling and happy.

Once the letter was finished, he put it into the envelope and lay in on the table, before taking a quick look around the room. He hadn't been in there before…it was lovely, warm and sunny with walls adorned with pictures painted by Tom Junior. The young boy had painted pictures of his family, and of the animals on the farm. Then, in one picture he'd drawn a huge ice-cream and labelled it 'my favourite food in all the world.'

Marco starred at it. He knew everything there was to know about ice cream. His father ran an ice cream parlour at home in Italy, and since he'd been a boy, he'd understood what it took to make the finest desserts in the country. Tom hadn't mentioned how much he liked ice cream before.

Marco desperately wanted to make them some of the delicious, natural ice cream that his father served in his shop. But would it be OK to use some of their precious milk? With rationing and scarce resources, he didn't know whether he should. Then he looked at the gorgeous picture again. He was sure they would be pleased if he left them a treat. So he headed outside and milked the goat, churning up the milk, freezing it then churning it again. He added nuts, berries and honeysuckle, and some icing sugar, mixing all the ingredients in a bag, then churning it, heating it, churning it, heating it, crushing it and leaving it in the freezer overnight with a note in his best handwriting, telling them what he had made for them. By the time he finished, he heard the sound of the truck at the gate, and rushed out of the farm house and down the long lane to join his fellow prisoners and head back to camp.

The next day when he arrived at the farm, Irene greeted him at the gate and gave him a huge hug. Marco noticed the admonishing looks from the soldiers on the truck. They hated the prisoners of war to get too close to the farmers they worked for, and particularly the farmers' wives and daughters.

"That was the loveliest ice cream I have ever tasted," she said, once the truck had trundled away. "It was amazing. How did you manage to make something so delicious without any ingredients?"

"It's like the ice cream my father makes in his cafe at home," he said. "I used to help him and I still remember how it was made. I used the things I found on the farm. I milked the goat. I hope that was OK?"

"Of course that was OK. It was very kind of you, and it was absolutely delicious. Can you believe that we ate half of it for breakfast? Tom Junior wouldn't relax until he'd tasted it. We've saved you some. Come in and have some ice cream."

Marco cautiously followed Irene, waiting at the farmhouse door, unsure whether he should go inside.

"Come in," she said. "Come on, you know everyone here."

"Hello, Marco," said Tom Junior whose face was covered in ice cream. The dogs had gathered around the table, hoping for scraps. Irene shooed them away and showed Marco to a seat, then she spooned more ice cream out for everyone and silence descended over the breakfast table as they enjoyed their indulgent treat.

"Do you know the story of Gelert the dog?" asked Tom Junior, looking up at Marco. "Daddy is going to tell me the whole story, right from the beginning. Do you want to hear it?"

"Ofcourse," said Marco, loving the way in which Tom Junior climbed onto his lap and looked up at him. He glanced up at Irene and Tom, as if seeking their approval for this. They both smiled.

"Right, well, Gelert was a lovely, kind dog who belonged to Tom the Great," started Tom Senior.

"Yes," said Tom, giggling to himself. He loved it when his dad changed the names in the stories they read together.

"The dog had been given to Tom the Great as a gift from Queen Irene of Carmarthen who was the most beautiful woman in all of Wales."

Irene shook her head and smiled at Marco.

"Except when she's cross," Tom Junior whispered. "She's not very beautiful when she's cross with me."

Marco laughed, and Tom Senior continued. "Well, this dog was a fine and loyal dog, and one day Tom the Great left the dog in the house with his baby, when he went out to do some farming. He thought the baby would be safe with the dog, but when Tom the Great returned, the baby was missing, the cradle had been overturned, and Gelert had blood all over his mouth.

"'You are a very naughty dog,' said Tom the Great, thinking that the dog had attacked the baby. 'Very, very naughty dog.'

"Tom the Great was so angry with the dog for killing his

baby that he pulled out his sword and killed the dog. Then, as soon as the dog was dead, Tom the Great heard his baby crying. The baby wasn't dead, he was hidden under the cot, completely safe. Next to the baby was a dead wolf.

"Tom the Great realised that the wolf had attacked the child and Gelert had killed the wolf and moved the baby to safety. Gelert the dog was a hero. Tom the Great was heartbroken by what had happened."

"Now make the story nice," said Tom Junior. "Make it nice like you did before."

"OK," said Tom Senior, as Marco ruffled the boy's hair. "Well, Tom the Great was horrified by what had happened and turned to look at the dog he had killed. He looked closer and realised the dog wasn't dead, his whiskers moved. Then the dog stood up…it was absolutely fine. Everyone was absolutely fine and Tom the Great was made king of all the world."

As Irene, Marco and Tom Junior cheered at the happy news, Marco heard the familiar rumbling of the truck pulling up the farm track towards the house.

"I wonder what they want?" said Marco, feeling nervous. Had they come to remove him from the farm because they saw him hug the farmer's wife? Or perhaps they heard that he had spent the previous afternoon making ice cream instead of working the land. He moved to stand up, but Tom beat him to it.

"You stay here," he said. "I will deal with them."

Minutes later, Tom came back in. "Well, Marco, it seems that Italy have changed their allegiance in the war. We're now all on the same side."

"Oh my," said Irene, while Marco sat there speechless.

"They can't repatriate everyone all at once, so it's been suggested that you stay working on the farm for now, until they know how your regiment will be redeployed for the Allies. I suggested to them that you come and live here, with us, and you'll be available for redeployment when the time comes. Does that sound OK?"

Marco dropped his head into his hands. He was overcome with joy.

"Please come and live with us. You can be my big brother," said Tom Junior.

"I'd love that," said Marco, turning to face Tom. "You've been incredibly kind to me right from the start. Thank you."

"You're welcome. Keith and Ken are moving back to work on their own farm because their father is ill, so we'll be busier than ever. Now go and write to your mother, tell her that this is your new address and she can always reach you here. I'll ring Llyr Beddows – the man who runs the local solicitors - and ask him what we have to do, legally, to make sure it's OK for you to stay here. He'll know…"

"Thank you," said Marco, hugging Irene and leaning over to shake hands with Tom. "You are incredibly kind people. I will never, ever forget what you have done for me."

Chapter 5

2018

"You're going for one night," said Ted, as he loaded my enormous case into the back of his car and walked over to sit in the driver's seat. "One night. Do you really need all this stuff?"

"I don't know," I said. The truth was that I had no idea what I needed or what was going to happen. I'd packed a black outfit to wear to the funeral, but besides that, I didn't know what we would be doing.

"I had to pack lots of things," I told Ted as he drove off towards the station. "What if I'm invited to a party or something?"

"It's a funeral. I don't think there'll be much partying going on."

"Ah, but we don't *know*, do we. I need to be prepared for

every eventuality. I need the right shoes for the occasion without having a remote clue what the occasion is."

Ted glanced at me despairingly as he cut through the early morning traffic.

"And it's a luxury hotel, remember, it's bound to have a lovely spa, so I've got all my gym and spa stuff so I can come back feeling all healthy."

"Why do they need you to be there today if the funeral isn't til tomorrow?"

"I don't know," I replied. "You spoke to the solicitor more than I did; I guess it's just to tell us about the guy that died and why we've all been invited. Hopefully by this evening I'll know what's going on."

"It's very intriguing," he said. "I'm still a bit worried though. You will be careful, won't you."

"It's very intriguing," I replied, ignoring the 'be careful' bit. "Mum's rung everyone in the family and no one has a clue who he is… This is all a complete bloody mystery. Dad's got no family at all really. As you know, his parents had him adopted when he was a baby. He has a half-brother who was adopted by a different family but the two fell out years ago and haven't spoken for – like – decades. It's so bloody complicated, but he says there was definitely no Reginald hovering around."

Ted dropped me at Esher station and from there I got a train to Reading and then on to South Wales. I'd never been to Wales before but I'd googled the place and it looked amazing. And I've watched lots of *Gavin and Stacey* and think Catherine Zeta-Jones is beautiful, so I was hopeful that I would enjoy it.

Having negotiated the first part of the journey with relative ease, I sat back on the train to Wales, shut my eyes, and thought about the bizarre scenario ahead of me.

Explaining to work why I couldn't come in had tied me up in the most ridiculous conversation.

"You don't know him, or you do know him?" Keith had asked, with understandable confusion.

"I don't know him, but I have to go to his funeral and while I'm there I assume I'm going to discover that I do know him, and I'll find out why."

"It seems odd," Keith said.

I told him he wasn't the first person to say that.

In the end I said I'd take three days off as holiday because I couldn't work out how I could claim them as bereavement days when I didn't even know the guy who had died and certainly couldn't claim he was a close relative. Luckily Keith had been quite enchanted by the mystery of it all and was very keen for me to go to find out what this was all about, so I only had to take two days holiday.

I opened my bag and laid out some snacks on the train table in front of me. I was determined not to eat like crazy this weekend; I was going off on a weight loss camp in a few weeks, and I had this idea (fantasy) of being able to slim down to a size 18 before I went (and – yes, I know what you're thinking, "Slim down to a size 18? That's not much of an ambition. What on earth size are you now?").

In answer to your questions: No, not much of an ambition, but an ambition nonetheless. I am a size 22, I convince myself that I'm a 20 but since I can't get into clothes that are size 20, it's an entirely inaccurate conviction.

I examined the snacks on the table before me and sighed. They looked so lovely, sitting there urging me to eat them all in one fell swoop. I'd bought a big bag of jelly babies because I read somewhere that jelly babies have absolutely no fat in them so footballers and rugby players eat them at half-time. I don't know whether this is true, and I'm fairly sure I don't want to look like a football or rugby player, but they must be quite good for you if nutritionists are letting leading sports people have them.

More importantly they tasted delicious – like sunshine had been melted down and shaped like babies. What's not to like about that?

I could resist it no more, I poured a pile of them into my hand and shoved them all into my mouth, feeling the gorgeous sugary taste as liquid fruitiness ran down the back of my throat. This is the problem with sweet stuff, isn't it? It tastes so bloody nice and makes you feel so wonderful.

I ate a Twix next then regretted it straight away and pushed the rest of my snacks into my handbag to take with me to the Gower Farm Hotel.

AT LLANELLI STATION I WAS THE ONLY PERSON TO GET OFF THE train, and I stepped onto the deserted platform like I was in some film from wartime... I was half waiting for the steam to clear to reveal my family, running towards me to greet me after I'd been away at war for years.

Sadly, there was no steam and no loving family waiting for me so I trundled along the platform, dragging my wheelie case behind me, and making a considerable racket as it bounced along on the uneven surface. They could probably hear me coming from half a mile away.

As I approached the main doors to the station, searching for Joe's Ice Cream Parlour, a kind-looking man dressed like an old-fashioned porter came out to see me and helped me with my bag, placing it in the boot of the taxi sitting outside with my name in the window.

"Have a lovely time, dear," he said in a beautiful Welsh accent, and I was driven away like I was a movie queen.

To say that the taxi took me out to the back of beyond would be to completely underplay the remoteness of the place I was taken to. Dear lord, we drove down tiny farm tracks where only one car would fit and had to pull over into the bushes if any other car came towards us. As we went along, the taxi driver told me tales of a tramp who once came and lay down on the ground in one of these lanes and was run over by a farmer's help in his tractor.

"Terrible business. We thought he'd be done for murder, we did," he said. "But they worked out the chap was dead before the tractor hit him. How do they work out that sort of thing?"

"Oh, I don't know," I said, surprised he'd taken me for someone with an in-depth knowledge of forensic medicine. "Perhaps they can tell how long the body's been dead?"

"How do they do that then?" he asked.

"Well, I'm not an expert, but I'm sure they can tell. I've seen *Miss Marple* lots of times and they can always tell when the person died. Perhaps they examine the contents of the stomach and can see how much food has been digested?"

"Good God, is that what they do, Miss Marple?" he said. "That's horrible if they do that, horrible."

"Yes, well, I suppose they have to find out the time of death to help them find out how someone died. My name's not Miss Marple, by the way. I think you got confused there."

"Right you are," he said. "We used to have lots of prisoners of war here during the war. It was probably one of them. Italians they were."

"Right." I wasn't sure how to respond to the snippets of local history being scattered in my direction, so we sat in an uncomfortable silence until he pulled into a narrow track leading up to a farm.

"I don't think I'm supposed to be staying at a farm," I said.

"No, this isn't a farm now. It used to be Gower Farm many years ago, but these days it's a very fine hotel. You'll like it."

"Oh good." I peered out of the window as we went past fields of sheep which gave the very distinct impression that this was, in fact, a farm. Then we went past hay barns and tractors and a chicken coop.

"You're absolutely sure that this isn't a farm?" I tried. I mean, I'm not a country girl but even I was able to discern farm-like features.

"Here we go then," he said. "This is the hotel I was told to bring you to." He beeped his horn loudly and the large front door creaked open. A woman came out and stood nervously next to the building that resembled, in every way, a farmhouse.

"This is Miss Marple," said the taxi driver.

"Oh, I thought you'd be Mary," said the lady, stepping slowly and cautiously towards me. "We're not expecting a Miss Marple. Have you booked?"

"I am Mary," I said. "There's been some sort of confusion about the name."

"There's your bag then, Miss Marple, enjoy your stay," said the taxi driver.

"Thank you," I said, flustered, as I tried to explain to this terribly kind Welsh lady in a brown cardigan and matching brown jumper that I wasn't Miss Marple and hadn't pretended to be Miss Marple, and I was, as she predicted, Mary Brown.

"Very well then," she said. "I'll call you Mary, if you don't mind. I'm Gladys. Come inside."

"Sure." I walked behind her, observing the flammable nest of a hairstyle, made rigid with so much hairspray that the slightest spark would have seen the whole thing go up in flames.

Chapter 6

DRAGGING MY LARGE BAG BEHIND ME, I TRAILED AFTER
Gladys, following the sway of her tweed skirt and the padding
of her sensible shoes on the ground, as she walked into the
reception area.

"You're staying on after the funeral, are you?" she asked in
quite a strong Welsh accent that I was really struggling to
understand. Then she looked at the size of my case. "I have
only booked you for one night. You plan to stay longer?"

"No, that's fine, one night is all I'm staying for," I said. I
found myself leaning into her in order to hear and understand
every word.

"You must be pissed here, after your long journey," she
said.

"Sorry?"

"I said 'you must be pleased to be here after your long
journey'."

"Oh, yes, pleased – yes, very pleased," I said, and I smiled and nodded warmly. This was going to be a fun couple of days.

"Is everyone else here?" I asked.

"Most of them are. Let me take you up to your room and you can freshen up, then come down for drinks before lunch in 20 minutes."

"OK," I said, walking up the stairs carpeted with some swirling monstrosity in faded yellow and brown. I followed Gladys to my room and watched as she opened it by clicking on the latch. No electronic key, not even a normal key.

"How do I lock my door?" I asked.

"There are no locks," said Gladys. "You're quite safe here. I'll see you downstairs soon."

The door emitted a creak like the whine of a dog in considerable distress as I pushed it wide open. I surveyed the heavily floral linen on the bed in the corner of the room. The flowers on the duvet were pale blue, the flowers on the wall were candyfloss pink, and underfoot were hideous swirls of brown and yellow. Never, in the history of womankind, have so many colours and patterns competed for attention.

I decided right there and then not to wear my fancy new bright green pyjamas for fear of burning a hole in the colour spectrum and finding myself dragged into it, never to be seen again.

There was a small dressing table in the corner that looked as if it had come from the early 20th century, horse brown and thickly lacquered. Like everything else in the room, it was in spectacularly bad taste.

Atop the table sat a gaudy old alarm clock, ticking loudly as if counting down to the end of the world.

It wasn't the sort of room one associated with a luxury hotel, in fact there was nothing about this place that brought to mind any thoughts of indulgence. I peered out of the small leaded windows at acres of fields, cranking one of them open to get a better look. It was beautiful outside, to be fair. Nothing but rolling fields as far as the eye could see.

I sat down heavily on the bed. This was obviously a beautiful part of the world, but this 'hotel' was nothing more than an old-fashioned farmhouse with none of the thrills or glamour that one would expect of even the most standard hotel. I did what I always did when feeling slightly disappointed or under pressure, and pulled out all the snacks I'd saved and laid them on the bed.

As I put my bag back down onto the floor, I noticed an envelope on the rather tatty bedside table. I picked it up and looked inside:

"Please meet downstairs for a late lunch at 3pm. Drinks will be served at 2.30pm," it said.

I looked from the note to my crisps and back again. It was almost lunchtime, I shouldn't eat anything really. But then again, circumstances like these allow for a little leeway, surely? I took some crisps out of the bag and crunched into them, feeling the gorgeous cheesy flavour fill my mouth. God, that was lovely. There was nothing quite as fabulous as food for making you feel instantly better, happier and more relaxed. The problem was that there was also nothing quite as effective as food for making you very, very fat.

I leaned my hands on my stomach which hung over the waistband of my trousers and instantly regretted the reckless snacking. I pushed against it, pulling my stomach in as much as possible, holding it in and saying a silent prayer that it would stay like that. The prayer didn't work though, it never does. I breathed back out and my stomach rolled over the top of my trousers again so I took another handful of crisps to escape the feeling of hopelessness.

Then I put my hand back into the envelope to recheck the timings on the note, and realised there were other pieces of paper in the envelope, including a letter in old-fashioned writing, the same writing as the letter that had been sent to me at home. Reginald's writing:

Dearest Mary,

If you are reading this note, you are here – in the Gower Farm Hotel. I'm so incredibly delighted. This was once a farm that meant so much to my father.

It's appropriate that you should be here because you mean so much to me. Everyone at this funeral means so much to me.

Your relative and the relatives of everyone here saved me from pain and misery and brought me to life again.

Reginald

What the hell?

I read the note again.

So, my relatives had helped him somehow. They'd saved him from pain and misery. There were other notes in the envelope. I loosened my trousers further, and sat back on the pillows. Tipping the contents of the envelope onto the bed.

There was list of everyone who was here and would be at the funeral along with photographs of them. I looked down the list at the unfamiliar names. At the bottom it said: "Tom Gower (not yet traced)." What did that mean? What did any of this mean?

Also in the envelope was an article about a writing course held in 1973.

It said: "Learn from one of the best teachers of playwriting in the world: Andrew Marks. Degree not essential but preferable." Then there were all the details of where the course would be taking place...in Bristol, of all places, at somewhere called the Bristol Playhouse.

Why would someone leave a cutting about a writing day course held in 1973? And how could it be so significant that it had caused him to invite six people he didn't know to his funeral?

I sat back on the bed, letting the notes and papers from the envelope fall onto the sheets next to me. My trousers were digging into me and my top was too thick in the warm room. I took my clothes off and lay on the bed in my bra and knickers, then I picked up the phone and rang Ted.

"So, who is he?" Ted sounded all excited. "Have you been told yet?"

"No, it's all getting weirder by the minute. This place doesn't look like a hotel at all – it's more like an old farmhouse – all creaky and old-fashioned."

"But you were told it was a luxury hotel – you took all your spa stuff. Is there no spa there?"

"Um, no," I said. "Nothing even remotely resembling a spa. We're in the middle of nowhere."

"And you think it's a farmhouse? Why do you say that?"

"Er...sheep, chickens and tractors everywhere."

"Yep, well, I guess that does make it sound like a farmhouse. Have you asked them why they said it was a luxury hotel?"

"No, I haven't seen anyone yet – only the lady on reception and I can barely understand a word she says. The accents they have here are so strong. I'm going down in 10 minutes to meet the others, but – get this – there's an envelope next to my bed, with an article in it about a writing course that was held in 1973. I think it's supposed to be some sort of clue, but I don't know how. Then there are details about the other people who will be here today."

"Oh, go on," said Ted. "Let me just get out of the office and I'll talk to you outside – tell me what it says."

I could hear Ted marching through the office as I told him about the contents of the envelope.

"Well, there's the advert for the creative writing course. I can't see any names on it that seem relevant, or any facts or figures that help me to understand this mad situation any better. I wonder whether the others have all got the same article as me? It might mean something to some of them."

"Gosh, Mary, that's so weird though. What was the name of the guy running the course? I'll google it, and see whether I can find anything out."

"Andrew Marks," I said, spelling it out.

"I'll check him out when I get off the. What else have you got?"

I told him all about the handwritten note, reading it out to him slowly as he wrote it down.

"I don't think that's a clue or anything. I think it's simply a note from him," I said.

"Yeah," Ted agreed. "I don't understand why they are giving you clues though, do you? Why not just bloody tell you who this guy was?"

"Well, that would be nice," I said. "They haven't told me anything more than the letter I got through the post told me. And the taxi driver thought I was Miss Marple."

"Miss who?"

"Marple – you know the TV detective."

"Oh, right. Why did they think that?"

"A bit of a language barrier, honestly, Ted, and the accents. The accent is impossible."

"And what about the others?" asked Ted, wisely opting not to grill me further on the circumstances that led to me being called Miss Marple. "Are they there yet?"

"Yes, they're here, but I haven't seen them yet. I'm upstairs in my room sitting on my bed."

"Go and find out who's there," said Ted. "Then it will all become clear. I wish I was there with you so I could help."

"I've got a list of who's here," I said. "But it doesn't really help very much because I've never heard of any of them."

"Ooooh...go through it. We need to work out what the link is between all the people there. I bet it'll be obvious whose funeral you're attending."

"Do you think?" I said. I wasn't at all convinced. But I did like Ted's childlike excitement about the whole thing. I reached over to pick up the piece of paper and stood it up on my stomach, leaning it against my thighs. My tummy was truly ridiculous, it was like it had a life of its own. I nudged it gently and watched as it rippled like a giant jelly; I swear to God it was a good five minutes before the rippling stopped.

"OK...well it says here that the people invited to the funeral are Matt Prior, who looks about 17 in the picture. He's doing a carpentry apprenticeship and lives in Wales."

"OK," said Ted, I could hear him scribbling down everything I said.

"Then there's Sally Bramley who looks a bit like my mum. I guess she's mid-50s. She's a PE teacher according to this, and she lives in Ascot."

"Right," said Ted.

"Then there's a Julie Bramley – I don't know whether she's related to the other Bramley but she's very glamorous. Works for a magazine in London. Looks like she's had a lot of work done. A bit like Pamela Anderson – you know – the one who used to be in *Baywatch*? And there are two more – Mike Sween – he's very handsome."

"Oh yeah," said Ted.

"No – I mean he's a handsome older man. He's, like, 50 or something – about my dad's age, so don't worry – but he looks like a TV presenter or an actor or something. He's got really dark hair that's probably dyed, and a dimple in his chin. He's from Wales, but now lives in Twickenham.

"Then there's a really old guy called Simon Blake. He's a theatre director and lives in Bath."

"Right."

There was an elongated pause while Ted was clearly thinking through the information I'd given him.

"So, there's a mixture of ages, genders, geographical locations and jobs? None of them have anything in common."

"Yep, that's about the size of it," I said.

"Mmmm... Although – hang on – read me the details of the playwrights' course you mentioned."

I pulled out the sheet and read it.

"Bristol?" said Ted.

"Yes," I replied.

"Isn't that near Bath?"

"I don't know. Why?"

"Well, didn't you say there was a theatre director there from Bath? He might have something to do with the playwrights' course?"

"Brilliant!" I said. "You should be a detective."

Chapter 7

1945

"HEY, YOU GUYS, COME HERE, COME HERE," SHOUTED IRENE, jumping up in the passenger seat of the tractor and waving her arms over her head, while Tom brought the vehicle to a stop. Marco ran across the field towards her, holding Tom Junior's hand.

"It's over. It's over. Germany has surrendered."

"What??" said Marco, stopping in his tracks.

"It's true. It's all over."

"Oh my God. Are you sure? Are you really sure?"

Marco threw Tom Junior into the air and shouted with joy.

"Remember it," he said to Tom Junior. "May 7th 1945. Never forget that, Tom. Will you? Remember it forever...the day the war ended."

He spun round, holding the young boy aloft. "Never forget it, Tom. Never."

The two of them climbed up and sat next to Irene on the tractor and they headed back to the farmhouse. "I won't forget it," muttered Tom Junior. Not in a million years.

Tom Junior was seven years old. He'd grown into a bright and inquisitive boy, helpful on the farm and hard-working at school. Marco knew he'd make a real success of his life. He wondered whether the boy would remember him, in the years to come. They had been in each other's lives so much for the past couple of years…seeing one another every day. Would he be remembered by any of these people? He knew he'd remember them forever.

"What are your plans then?" asked Tom when they arrived back in the farmhouse kitchen.

"I guess I'll go back to Italy," said Marco, though he felt so sad at the thought of leaving Llanelli. He was looking forward to seeing his parents, but leaving this beautiful part of the world that he'd made home didn't appeal at all.

"Have you been writing to your mother regularly?"

"Yes," said Marco, though the truth was he'd only sent a few letters even though he'd received loads from his mum.

"Write to her. Invite her to visit us with your father," said Tom. Irene turned and smiled at her husband. He wasn't normally as sociable, and he didn't extend invitations easily, but she knew how much he had come to love Marco, and didn't want him to leave. Marco was a joy around the house as well as being so incredibly helpful on the farm.

"Yes," agreed Irene. "Please invite them, Marco. That would be lovely. And invite your friend Lorenzo – we haven't seen him for a while."

AND SO, FOUR WEEKS LATER, HIS MOTHER AND FATHER ARRIVED

on the farm. They looked so out of place – his mother, Anna, with a shawl around her shoulders, and his father knowing only a handful of English words. Anna gasped when she saw her son – bigger, stronger and more handsome than ever. She threw herself into his arms, sobbing and overcome with joy.

He introduced his parents to the couple who'd become his surrogate parents, and to Tom Junior who clung onto Marco as if he thought they'd come to take him away.

"We've organised a little party for you tonight," Marco told them. "So you can meet the new friends I've made here." He spoke in Italian which felt somehow strange after so many years of speaking English and struggling to understand Welsh.

"There's no need. Tell them not to go to so much trouble," his mum said. Marco knew that his mum wasn't much of a party animal and was aware that being the centre of attention at a party thrown in her honour would be very daunting, but he also knew how keen Tom and Irene were on welcoming them properly.

Despite Anna's resistance to the idea, by 7pm the following evening, Gower Farm had been transformed. Fairy lights dazzled and balloons danced as music filled the air. Marco had made loads of delicious ice cream, there were sandwiches aplenty and stacks of Welsh cakes. He'd not seen such a spread since before the war. The party was to celebrate the end of the conflict and the visit of Marco's parents. Tom and Irene were determined to make it the best party ever, and locals drifted in through the evening – all carrying parcels of food to add to the collection, and bottles of beer to share.

Marco walked round checking that everyone was OK, and introducing his mother and father to all the people he had come to know so well while in Wales. His parents smiled as introductions were made, but he knew how shy they felt being paraded around, so once they had met everyone, he took them back over to Tom and Irene, and gave them all chairs to sit on, so they could chat comfortably, away from the madding crowd.

"I'll see you later. You all behave yourselves now. No getting into trouble while my back's turned," he said, jokingly.

"Not like we used to then," said a voice behind him. He swung round. His great friend, Lorenzo, was walking through the party with the trademark swagger that took Marco straight back to memories of their youth together.

"Lorenzo. This is magical. Come here."

Marco pulled Lorenzo into a warm hug.

"So good to see you," said Lorenzo. "How's everything been?"

"It's great. Tom and Irene have been brilliant. I've stayed working on the farm. I couldn't be happier. How about you?"

"I've been OK. I moved off the farm I was on, and have been working in Swansea. Do you know it? It's not far from here."

"I've heard of it," said Marco. "Come on, let's get you a beer."

The two men walked over to the small disused hen-house near the main house. It had been converted into a bar and dance hall for the evening. Marco reached for a beer and turned to hand it to his friend.

Then, he saw her. The most beautiful sight his eyes had ever fallen upon – a gorgeous raven-haired woman – small, slight and delicate, standing near the door, gazing out into the warm summer's evening. Marco stood and stared for a while.

"Am I going to get that beer?" asked Lorenzo.

"Sure. Here you go."

"Who's the girl you keep starring at?"

"I don't know. I've never seen her before."

"Go and talk to her," he said. It was just like the old days, when the two of them would cruise around the coffee bars on their scooters, looking for girls to chat to.

But it was so much harder now. He felt like a different person since the war…more serious, less able to engage in flippancy and playfulness.

"I don't know how to," said Marco.

"I do." Lorenzo walked straight up to the girl and put his hand out.

"I'm Lorenzo, this is my friend Marco. He's famous in Italy. His dad makes the best ice cream in the country."

"Nice to meet you," said Marco, his face burning with embarrassment.

"Can I get you a drink or anything?"

"I'm fine," she said. "But thank you."

"I'll see you later," said Lorenzo, walking away, whistling to himself as he clutched his beer in his hand, and headed outside.

"I live here with Tom and Irene," Marco said. "What's your name?"

The lady went bright red. "I'm Madelyn."

She spoke with a strong Welsh accent. Marco knew that if they'd met when he first came to the country, he would never have understood her. Now though, he understood everything she said.

"Do you live locally?"

"I am on the farm on the other side of the valley. I live with my mum and dad, and my brothers – Ken and Keith. They used to work on the farm. I think you know them."

"Ken and Keith? Yes, I know them. They were here when I first arrived. They left not long afterwards."

"They used to talk about you," she said. "They told me how nice you were."

"That's good of them. Are they here today? I'd love to say hello."

"No, they're on the farm. They are running it together because dad got ill and couldn't do any physical work anymore."

"I'm sorry to hear that. Tell them I said hello."

"Of course I will, and can I change my mind about that drink?"

"Yes, what do you fancy?"

And that was it.

Marcus and Madelyn spent the entire evening together and Marco was smitten. It turned out that Madelyn was just a year younger than him and had been born on Dirgelwch Farm where she'd lived all her life, and now worked, organising the sales from the farm shop they had set up even though they had so little produce to sell to customers it had become ridiculous.

"I spend most of my time telling people we don't have what they want. Hopefully that will change now the war is over."

Marco looked into eyes of melted chocolate and knew, without a shadow of a doubt, that he would marry this woman.

Chapter 8

1950

"WHAT'S BACIO?" ASKED THE LITTLE BOY WITH BRIGHT BLONDE hair, standing on tiptoes to peer into the glass-fronted cabinet, while his mother stood beside him.

"He loves your ice cream," she explained. "He can't get enough of it."

"I am glad. Well, bacio means 'kiss'," said Madelyn, offering the boy an air kiss and seeing his nose wrinkle in disgust.

"I don't want a kiss, I want an ice cream."

"Stop teasing the customers," said Marco, appearing at his wife's side and draping his arm over her shoulder before addressing the boy. "So, little man – this is how it works in this ice cream shop: on this side of the cabinet we have the 'fruits of the farm' ice creams which are made from fruits and nuts grown at Gower Farm. On this side are the 'taste of Italy' ice creams – coffee, chocolate, vanilla, and fudge…things like that…flavours that we have a lot of in Italy. Now, if you want a mixture of flavours you have a bacio – a kiss of flavours. So you could have hazelnut and chocolate or toffee…whatever you fancy. If you want three flavours it's a bacio grande – a big kiss – and four flavours is a neopolitan."

"Dad, Dad," shouted the boy. "Please can I have a big kiss?"

Madelyn smiled as she saw the expression of surprise on the face of the boy's father, before the two of them ordered a bacio grande comprised of the sweetest flavours they could find.

The place had been buzzing all day, but it was mainly locals who came. Because the ice cream shop was based on Gower Farm, it was hard to alert people to the fact that the cafe was there. Madelyn had done her best, and had hung bunting at the end of the farm track, and put notes in the windows of the newsagents in Llanelli telling everyone that a new ice cream shop had opened selling all natural ice cream with fresh milk, but it was very difficult to be sure that passers-by knew about them.

At 10pm, they shut the shop and cleaned the floors, making sure that all the ingredients were ready for ice cream making the next morning. They'd fallen very comfortably into a routine of hard work and determination to make their ice cream shop the best in the world.

"As long as we make ice cream that tastes great, is reasonably priced, and is served with a smile, we will make a success of this," Marco was fond of saying. "We have to."

"Is all the fruit cleaned and ready?" asked Madelyn, as Marco did his final checks.

"Yes, all ready," he said.

"Come on then you, let's go to bed."

Their life was busy but enjoyable and Marco thanked his lucky stars every day that he'd found himself working on Tom's farm when he'd been captured during the war.

He and Tom hadn't been in each other's pockets quite so much since the ice cream shop opened, but they still enjoyed one another's company and Madelyn would often take a tub of ice cream round to the family, and chat to Irene over a cup of tea and a bacio grande.

On Friday night they had Tom and Irene coming over for dinner, and Madelyn was determined to make a huge success of it. She and Marco had exciting news to share with their landlords and she wanted to cook a perfect Italian dinner over which to tell them. She bought all the ingredients necessary and they had hired staff to cover them in the shop in the evening so they could entertain properly.

Madelyn slipped upstairs to change before dinner, while Marco went over to the ice cream parlour to check everything was OK. At 8pm on the dot, Irene and Tom arrived.

Marco poured a small sherry for Irene and gave Tom a beer.

"The ice cream parlour has been packed recently," said Marco. "Thank you for allowing us to set up shop on the farm."

As Marco spoke, he saw Tom glance over at Irene and then look away quickly, but it was enough of an eye movement to let Marco know that something was afoot.

"Is everything OK?" asked Marco. "I get the feeling there might be something wrong."

"Not wrong, as such," said Tom, as Madelyn encouraged them to take their seats for dinner. "It's just…ahhh…I don't know how to say this…we've decided to retire, to sell the farm and move to North Wales where Irene's parents live. They're getting old and I think it's time we looked after them. Obviously, if we sell the farm, we'll be selling your shop with it. We've talked to Llyr Beddows and looked at whether we can sell you the shop separately so you'd own that bit of the building, but it's all integral to the farmhouse and the likely buyers are keen to turn the farm into a hotel – Gower Farm Hotel they want to call it. I'm afraid that when we sell the farm, we'll be selling your shop with it. I'm sorry. There's nothing we can do."

Marco felt his heart sink, but Tom had done so much for them, he didn't want him to feel guilty about leaving. "Don't worry, you've given us the best start ever – we've got a thriving business and a loyal customer base, it's about time we moved to the High Street and tried to make a go of it independently. I'm sorry you're moving away though. That's very sad. Very sad indeed."

Tom leaned over, took the bottle of sherry and topped up Irene's glass. "You're not drinking, Madelyn?"

"No, not tonight," she said, glancing at Marco.

It was Tom's turn to be concerned. "I saw that glance," he said. "What aren't you telling us?"

"I'm pregnant," said Madelyn with an enormous smile. "We're going to have a baby."

"Oh, that's wonderful news," said Irene, leaping up and hugging the young woman who'd become like a daughter to her. "I'm so pleased for you both, you'll make the most wonderful parents. Oh Tom, now I'm heartbroken that we're moving away. You two don't fancy coming to Llandudno with us, do you? It's a very lovely place with beautiful beaches and spectacular cliffs. We could help you set up an ice cream shop there – it'll be perfect for all the tourists passing through."

"We can't," said Marco, shaking his head. "This place means so much to me. I love it here. I couldn't bear to leave."

"We'll help you relocate the shop," said Irene.

"But don't worry, we'll be fine, won't we, love? As long as we make good ice cream, sell it at reasonable prices and serve it with a smile, we'll always be all right. And we're going to have a child…maybe it will be a son, and we will call him Joe. And when we open our ice cream shop we'll call it Joe's Ice Cream Parlour."

"That's a lovely idea," said Irene, offering a smile tinged with sadness.

"Tell me about the farm – how are they going to change it into a hotel?" asked Madelyn, eager to stop her husband from becoming too excited about the prospect of a son. She could have a daughter, and she wanted Marco to love a girl just as much.

"I think the plan is for them to keep it so it still has a farm-house feel, with lovely fields outside, animals and some of the farming outbuildings, and making it as authentic as possible inside, but obviously modernised. We have six bedrooms remember, plus there's a big attic and lots of big rooms down-stairs. They are convinced it will work."

Marco looked at the old dresser with the plates sitting on it, plates with pictures of scenes from the local area as well as produce prepared in the farmhouse going back decades – there was a plate depicting a picture of the castle, flowers and plants. One had a couple of lamb chops and potatoes on it which looked exactly like the dinners he'd had on the farm when he'd moved in with them years ago. It seemed such a shame that it would no longer be here as a working farm. He'd devoted so much time to it – sweated blood on that land. "Won't you miss it?" he asked Tom.

"Desperately," he replied. "But it's the right thing to do."

Chapter 9

2018

It was time for me to go down to meet this rather disparate group of people. On the surface it seemed they had nothing in common with me, but presumably I was about to discover the golden thread that bound us together, and to Reginald.

I wasn't sure what I was in for, and though I'm a confident person, a feeling of nervousness crept over me as I walked along the creaky old corridor towards the stairs. The walls were slightly wonky and the floor was uneven under the hideously patterned carpet beneath my feet. Crockery plates adorned the walls, all of them featuring scenes from the local area; a castle, beach scenes, flowers and plants. I walked past them, inspecting every one of them, hoping to distract myself from the nervousness growing inside me. One of the plates featured a couple of lamb chops and potatoes. How completely weird. Why on earth would you want a picture of your dinner on the wall?.

I turned the corner and saw the wide staircase I'd come up earlier. Thank God. Without any discernible sense of direction to rely on, it was always a moment of wonder when I discovered I was going the right way. The stairs seemed odder walking down than they had seemed when I came up – like I was descending into some terrible B-movie in which sinister women with their hair in buns would stare at me while stirring pots of boiling water. At the bottom of the stairs, I walked across the oak entrance hall searching for the right room. Then I saw it – a small sign on one of the doors 'Friends of Reginald Charters'. That had to be it. I wasn't sure I qualified as a friend, but I pushed open the large door and peered inside. Lots of faces turned to stare at me. They looked as confused as I felt.

"Hi, I'm Mary," I said, with a smile. "Anyone got a clue what's going on here?"

A RATHER ELEGANT-LOOKING MAN WALKED OVER AND SMILED warmly.

"Welcome," he said. "And no, none of us has the remotest clue what's going on, darling. It's most baffling." He had an aristocratic, slightly theatrical air and I decided this must be Simon Blake. He was a director and looked every inch his profession, with thinning blonde hair that I suspect was once his crowning glory. Now he clung onto it like a drowning man clinging to a life raft. Every hair seemed to be coiffured and styled to within an millimetre of its life.

He wore a rather shabby, but expensive-looking, linen jacket in a creamy beige colour over green cords, a light blue shirt and navy blue jumper. It was an odd assortment. He was a handsome man, older, and a little frail but still good-looking. He was far too thin though, he could do with eating more, but I wasn't going to start advising him on his calorie intake. I think I was about three times his circumference. He had a warm smile and a nice demeanour. And he'd made the effort to come over and talk to me while the others just stared fearfully, as if I'd entered the room carrying a Kalashnikov.

"Mary, join us for tea and let me introduce you to everyone here. As you can imagine, we're all trying to work out why we've been gathered in this room, and what on earth it is that we've got in common. Perhaps you will be the missing piece in the jigsaw that allows us to solve this conundrum."

"I do hope so," I said. "I've never been a jigsaw piece before."

I saw the tea on the side – a lovely big, old-fashioned teapot with a floral pattern on it, but also saw a bottle of wine. I would have much preferred a glass of wine, but there were biscuits with the tea, and I am very, very fond of biscuits. Would it be acceptable to have a glass of wine and a short-bread biscuit? I decided this was not an appropriate course of action, so I had a cup of tea that I didn't want so I could have the biscuit that went with it. Then I instantly regretted my choice.

"Would it be rude to ask for wine instead of tea?" I said. "This is such an odd situation; I feel like a little glass would help me to relax."

"Of course, it's not a problem," said Simon, turning his back to pick up the bottle, thus allowing me a moment to reach over and grab a biscuit.

"Let's get this bottle of wine open," he said.

It was at that point I realised no one else was drinking alcohol. They hadn't even opened the bottle. What sort of people were they?

"Oh no, don't open it just for me. I'll have tea," I said, hoping to God he didn't take me at my word.

"No, no, if you want a little glass of wine, you shall have a little glass of wine. I'm sure I'm capable of getting this bottle open." He then proceeded to make an inordinate fuss about going through the drawers of a big oak dresser and trying to summon assistance to find a bottle opener.

"Bottle opener? Bottle opener?" he shouted through the room.

A young man who'd been looking at the farm pictures on the far side of the room walked towards us. He was handsome and muscular. He leant over and gently unscrewed the top of the wine bottle and handed it to Simon. "There you go," he said. "It's a screw top."

"Yes, of course, yes," said Simon, adjusting a cravat that he wasn't wearing and running his hands through his manicured hair. "Now then, all we need is a glass."

As he looked around, frantically surveying the room in search of a glass, the handsome young man stood before him, holding one. Eventually Simon realised, and took it, looking quite emasculated in the process.

"I'm Matt," the young man said to me in a gentle Welsh accent. "Very nice to meet you." He went bright red as he spoke and appeared nervous despite his tough-looking shell.

"It's lovely to meet you too," I said. "Would you like to join me in a glass of wine?"

"I don't drink," said Matt. "It makes me ill. But if I did, I would definitely join you."

I smiled at him; how polite he was. But fancy not drinking? That was odd. When I was his age the contents of my veins were 80% alcohol. I thought back to the list of people who'd be here today…this had to be Matt Prior. He was in his late teens according to the notes I'd been left, but he looked older in the flesh, quite different form his picture, perhaps early 20s, but seemed so shy, so nervous while he was talking to me.

As Simon handed me the glass of wine, the door opened and a very attractive woman walked in. Gosh. She was tall and slim in a tight-fitting cashmere skirt and jumper combination, and an elaborate collection of gold and pearl necklaces hung around her neck. She was so beautiful and with the tiniest waist I'd ever seen. I put down my biscuit as a sign of respect. You know how people say "she was really attractive but she just didn't know it"? Well, this woman was the opposite of that. She was beautiful and boy did she know it.

She walked in, oozing confidence and sophistication, sashaying through the room, making cold eye contact with everyone as they turned one by one to stare at her. Every inch of carpet she stepped onto became her runway. She was beautiful in a way that made it impossible for me to stop looking at her, she seemed to have been put together better than anyone else in the room.

She was the sort of person who everybody wanted to befriend, to have in their social circle, in their orbit, so they could feel touched a little by the beauty radiating from her. But, although we all watched her as she walked across the room, she never acknowledged any of us, she let her big blue eyes flick from person to person, but she wasn't looking at us, she was checking whether we were looking at her.

The woman moved to the back of the room, slightly away from us but still within earshot, and peered out of the window as if searching for something far more interesting than any of us could provide.

I smiled at her and she smiled back but it was only her lips that curved into the shape of a smile while her face stayed stationary. It wasn't a smile to embrace you but a smile to distance you and keep you down where you belonged.

"This is all rather tiresome," she said. "Does anyone know what the hell is going on?"

"Hopefully we will soon," I said, eager to make her happy. I always do this with good-looking people. There's a guy called Dave who lives in the flat below me, and I fall apart whenever he talks to me. He's not particularly interesting, but I fall at his feet and would do anything for him (literally – honestly – the things I've done would make you blush!).

"We haven't met," said the beautiful woman. "I'm Julie."

She pronounced her name as if she were French: Zjoolieeee, drawing out the final vowel.

I just stared at her.

"And you?" she said.

"Oh. Sorry. I'm Mary Brown." I put out my hand to shake hers, almost curtseying in the process, but she'd turned away and was ferreting in her expensive-looking handbag. The bag might have been from Top Shop for all I knew, but it looked exquisite and costly…everything about this woman looked really expensive. "We've been told that lunch is in half an hour, and that we might like to chat amongst ourselves about the funeral, and the guy who has died."

"Yes, isn't it utterly daft? Though I understand we're in for some money. Does no one here know him?" she said. "I mean – surely one of us has a clue who this guy was?"

I felt overwhelmed with excitement that she'd chosen me to talk to. Me!

"None of us has a clue," said Simon, coming over to join us. "Not the remotest clue."

Chapter 10

THE MORE I LOOKED AROUND THE PEOPLE GATHERED IN THE room, the more I felt like I was in an elaborate Agatha Christie movie. All we needed was the arrival of Hercule Poirot for us to be in a Christmas Special on the BBC. There was the beautiful but brittle woman in Julie, the very handsome and terribly nice younger man, and the theatrical older man. If Christie had plotted this, Julie would definitely be the one who murdered Reginald. Or was that too obvious? Perhaps it would be the daft fat woman in the corner drinking wine and eating biscuits?

"I'm Sally," said an older woman, interrupting my fantasies. I'd missed her arrival in the room because I'd been so fascinated by Julie. Sally was quite plain and sturdy and immediately reminded me of a cross between my mum and Clare Balding. "I'm Julie's sister."

"Oh, lovely to meet you," I said. "Which Julie's your sister?"

"Julie, there," she pointed to the crazily beautiful woman

who was heading towards the doors that led outside. "The woman you were talking to earlier."

I was open-mouthed.

"I know – we don't look alike – she got the good looks; I got the good personality. What can you do?"

"Ha!" I laughed and thought immediately that no amount of lovely personality would compensate for not looking like Julie.

Her sister's exit through the back doors, presumably to smoke or get some fresh air, was done with exactly the same dramatic flounce that had accompanied her entrance.

The atmosphere in the room shifted a little when she left, a kind of calmness descended. Simon walked towards me, refilling my glass (I don't know what happened to that first glass – it seemed to disappear).

"Did you get the cuttings on your bed?" asked Sally.

"Yes," I said, moving to pull them out of my bag. "I've got them with me. Did you get some too?"

"Yes, I think we all got them. I spoke to Simon earlier and he suggested that we all go through them and compare notes over lunch. We should be able to work out who this guy was, and then we'll all feel a bit more comfortable about everything."

"Yes!" I replied. She had hit the nail on the head – we'd all feel so much better and more relaxed about everything once we knew who he was. It was hard to feel calm about a situation when you had no idea why you were in it.

"Does anyone have any ideas at all at the moment?" I asked.

Sally and Simon both shook their heads. "No one I've spoken to has ever heard of this guy," said Sally. "I've talked to my relatives and he's definitely nothing to do with my family.

I'm a school teacher and I've been back through the lists of children who went to the school, in case one of their parents is related to this guy. I just can't find any link at all."

"Me neither," said Simon. "I'm completely baffled."

"He's definitely not related to me," I said. "I don't know why I'm here. I'm sure they're going to discover they've invited me by mistake, and they were after another Mary Brown. It's such a common name. I can't believe I was really invited by this guy on his deathbed. How would that ever happen to someone like me?"

"That's exactly what I thought," said Sally. I felt myself warming to her. "I was talking to my friend last night and I said to her that I fully expect them to announce halfway through that they got the wrong person."

"It's interesting that you and your sister have been invited though, isn't it?" I said. "It makes it sound like there must be a reason in your family for you to have been invited, rather than any of the students at school."

"Yes, I guess so, but I spent all of yesterday with Mum while she phoned around, and we are absolutely sure he's not related to us."

Julie came back into the room, smelling strongly of perfume, her lips glistening with lipstick that she had obviously freshly applied after her cigarette.

"Shall we see if we can sit down for lunch," she said. "There is no point standing around here any longer than necessary."

"I think someone is still missing," said Simon. He appeared to be taking on a leadership role. You know how when group of people are thrown together, one person emerges as leader? Well that was definitely Simon in this little group. I felt he would be the one to solve the conundrum of who Reginald was and why we were all called here today.

"I'll just check who's still to come," he said, consulting a piece of paper. "A guy called Mike Sween is missing. It says on here that he might be 10 minutes or so late."

"Well he's about half an hour late now," said Julie. "Why don't we just go through and get started on this. I've got a few calls I need to make and I don't want to spend all evening faffing around waiting for late-comers."

"Sure. There's nothing to stop us going through and sitting at the table and having a chat," said Simon. "But I'm sure they won't serve lunch til everyone is there."

"Come on then," said Julie. "I might as well lead the way."

I glanced at Simon and he shrugged at me. Letting Julie do exactly what she wanted was going to be a theme of the day.

Chapter 11

"SHALL I BE CHAIRMAN?" ASKED SIMON AS WE ALL TOOK OUR seats at a long, sombre-looking, uninspiring, table.

"Sure," I said, reaching over to take a bread roll from the tureen in the middle. "That would be good."

I just wanted us to solve the mystery of why we were there. If Simon wanted to take on the bulk of the responsibility, it was fine by me. I bit into my bread roll. It wasn't half as nice as it looked. The thing was solid all the way through. I struggled to hide my disappointment. There is little in life as annoying to me as bad food.

"Should we not vote? I mean – you can't cast yourself in the role of team leader without us all agreeing," said Julie.

"OK. We'll have a vote. If anyone else wants to do it, that's fine by me. I think we need someone, anyone, coordinating things."

There was a silence in the room.

"Anyone like to put their name forward?" he asked.

More silence.

"Well, shall I do it then?"

There were murmurs of encouragement while Julie sat back heavily in her seat and crossed her arms.

She was starting to look less attractive as the day wore on.

"Right, OK then. Look – I'm no wiser than any of you as to why we've been gathered here today. Clearly the man who died feels he knows us in some way, and wants us to work out how. Now, what I suggest we do is–"

But before Simon could finish his sentence, the big, oak doors at the far end of the room squeaked open and three men came in. The first of the men was exquisitely handsome and beautifully dressed – he looked like an actor or a model or something. That must be Mike Sween. I watched Julie eye him up, and preen herself as he walked past. Behind him strode two older men, one clutching a briefcase, the other holding loose notes in his hand.

"Mike, why don't you take a seat," said the man with the briefcase, laying his things down on the table and waiting for the guy with the notes to join him.

"Ladies and gentlemen, thank you so much for coming here today," he said, in a soft, Welsh accent. "My name's Huw and this is Geraint. We are from Beddows and Plunkett Solicitors and we are handling the estate of Mr Reginald Charters."

I put the stale bread roll back down onto my plate. This was serious.

"I know this is all very strange, and most of you who I have talked to during the week expressed your surprise and confusion about what is going on here. I'm going to be honest and say that Geraint and I have been working as solicitors in this town for almost 40 years and we have never known anything like this. We will run through everything we know, and explain as best we can what will be happening over the next 24 hours. OK?"

"Fine," said Julie. "But you must realise that this is all a little tiresome. I'm not a child. I have no desire to play silly games. I hope you're able to tell us precisely what is happening."

"We'll do our best," said Huw, opening his briefcase and taking out some notes. "Geraint, is there anything you want to say at this stage?"

"No," said Geraint, blushing furiously and speaking in a very strong Welsh accent. "Nothing to add."

"OK, well there are six of you here. You have been explicitly invited by Mr Charters who died a few days ago of natural causes and was very keen for you to come to Wales for the weekend and attend his funeral.

"He was explicit in his instructions, leaving your addresses and lots of detail about you with a private detective who passed them onto us. He wanted to ensure that we invited the right people. Mr Charters wanted you, and only you, to come to the funeral. At this stage in the proceedings I am instructed to read this note:

HELLO DEAR FRIENDS,

A MOST HEARTY WELCOME TO GOWER – ISN'T IT BEAUTIFUL? I'M sorry I'm not there with you but I've gone and stumbled into an untimely death. I'm a very rich man and have a lot of money to give away...I'd like to give the money to you all. How about that?

. . .

But before I do that, I want you to guess why you've been brought here…why have I requested your presence out of all the people in all of the world? Try and work it out. I've left you all clues.

You'll be handsomely rewarded if you work it out. There's £1 million up for grabs if you can work out why you're here.
Yours,

Reginald

There was a little shuffling and murmuring at that point. Was he suggesting that we would inherit a load of money but only if we could work out why we were there?

"That's all the note says… I'll leave it for you to mull over. As I said, we really don't know why you've been called here and it seems he wanted you to try and work that out. We were merely instructed to make sure that you were present and that all expenses were covered and you were treated like royalty.

"The funeral is tomorrow morning and after that I would like to welcome you to our office in the High Street for a will reading and the showing of a video prepared by Mr Charters. I suspect that is when the full reasons for your presence here will be revealed.

"Now my partner Mr Geraint Plunkett will talk you through the funeral arrangements."

"Well, yes," said Mr Plunkett. He was scarlet, poor man, and in his embarrassment, he had retreated further into a thicker Welsh accent than any of us could understand.

"Could you just say that again?" asked Simon politely.

"We can't understand any of this," said Julie, slightly more aggressively.

"Anyone want to have some egg and cress?" he said, louder than before, hoping we could all understand him. "It's very important for someone to have it."

To be honest, I was famished. There was no immediate danger of any lunch being served, the rolls were rock hard and I do like egg and cress sandwiches.

"Me," I said, raising my hand and smiling at him.

"Are you sure?" said Simon, lightly touching my arm. "That's quite a lot to expect of you. To be honest, I think it's pretty awful of them to ask."

"No, I don't mind at all," I said. "Very, very happy indeed."

"Diolch," said Geraint, before quickly saying, "Sorry – I mean, thank you."

Then Huw explained that we'd have our lunch now. I did wonder how my egg and cress sandwiches fitted into all this talk of lunch, but I decided not to ask.

Talking much more slowly, as if explaining something to a recalcitrant toddler, Geraint continued.

"In the morning you'll head over to the chapel at 9.30am. Mary, I'll come and collect you at 9am, so that you can see the church beforehand and have time for a quick practice there."

"Practice there?" I said.

"Yes, before you give the head address."

"Head address?"

"Yes – you just said you'd like to give the address…at the funeral."

"No I didn't."

"Yes you did, just now," interrupted Simon. "They asked who wanted to do it and your hand shot up."

"Oh. The address? Oh, I see. Right, yes of course."

Not egg and cress but a fucking address. How had this happened? Why was everyone so Welsh? I just couldn't understand half of what was being said. No wonder Simon had expressed reservations when I raised my arm.

"I'll leave you to have lunch and I look forward to seeing you all bright and early in the morning. Once again, I'm sorry I have no way of letting you know any more about this rather surreal situation, but I'm sure everything will become clearer as you talk tonight."

With that, the two men smiled, turned and left.

"The address?" I said to Simon. "How can I give an address about a man I don't know?"

"Well, I did wonder," he said. "I couldn't quite believe it when you volunteered so readily."

"That's because I thought he said 'who wants egg and cress?'. For the love of God – I thought he was offering sandwiches."

Chapter 12

"Maybe we should start with you then, Mary," said Simon. "Do you want to tell us a little about yourself and run through what was in your cuttings envelope? I'll write it down in this notebook and at the end we'll try and make sense of how everyone's stories dovetail together and what that tells us about Reginald. Does that sound sensible to everyone?"

"It seems pointless, not sensible," said Julie. "What do you think, Mike?"

"Oh, um. I don't know. I've just sat down. I think it would be useful to try and work out why we're here and who this guy was before the funeral tomorrow though, especially if there's money at stake."

"OK, well, Mary, kick us off. Tell us a little bit about yourself."

"My name is Mary Brown and I live in a place called Cobham in Surrey," I said. "I work at a DIY and gardening centre, and I don't like it very much. And… I'm not sure what else to say. I have a friend called Dawn who runs a blog, and I sometimes do vlogs for her, including once going to South Africa on safari and once I went on a cruise. That's the only stuff really that's got me into the public eye. No, actually – that's not true. Once I had a bit of an incident with David Beckham's Christmas tree that meant me ending up in the papers and on *This Morning*. But that was a couple of years ago now. Basically, I don't do anything very remarkable, I just go to work and get drunk with my friends and my boyfriend, and I've no idea on earth why I'm here."

"OK, thank you, Mary. Maybe we'll come back to the David Beckham connection if it turns out it's significant when everyone else does their little talk. Do you want to run through what's in your envelope?"

"Yes – of course," I said. "Although it doesn't seem to make a great deal of sense to me. I have a flyer advertising a playwriting course at Bristol Playhouse in 1973."

"Interesting. Does it say who was running the course, Mary? Was it Reginald, by any chance?"

"A man called Andrew Marks," I said. "There is no mention of Reginald anywhere in the cutting, and I even googled the course and couldn't find any mention of it."

"Perhaps it would be worth you reading out what's on the sheet."

I went through it, relaying all the information.

"OK, I've got that written down. Is there anything else in your envelope?"

"No," I said. "Well, nothing else except a note from Reginald and a list of everyone who's here today. That's it."

I read out the letter Reginald had left and it became clear that everyone had received the same letter – all handwritten.

"Maybe I should go next," said Simon. "Because I think the playwriting course might tie in with my family in some way... I have worked as a theatre director in Bath for many years, and Bath is not that far from Bristol."

His news drew gasps from the assembled group, and a little muttering. None of us had expected to be able to work out who on earth this guy was, but now, suddenly, it felt like we might. There was a shiver of excitement at the prospect. Was the story of Reginald Charters tucked away somewhere in the world of drama and theatre?

"So," said Mike. "Let me get this straight – so far we know that Reginald is somehow connected to a playwriting course at Bristol Playhouse in the 1970s and that links Mary to him, and Simon is a theatre director nearby. That's all quite interesting."

"But it was before I was born," I said. "How could I possibly be linked to it?"

"Maybe not you, but a member of your family? Make a note to check with someone in your family about whether they ever lived in Bristol, Mary."

"Sure," I said, though I was fairly sure my mum had never even been to the theatre let alone attended theatre writing courses on the other side of the country. I'm sure I'd know if we had a famous relative.

"Let me run through my cutting then," said Simon.

"Mine says 1977 on the top and it's a list of four different plays, all written by different people and performed all over the country. I've googled the playwrights but can't access any decent information on them, which I'm surprised about.

"My father was a theatre producer at a number of theatres and I think these plays might have been put on in theatres he was based in, or overseeing, but that's all.

"I've definitely seen *A Bit of a Puzzler* – that's a great play – written by some guy called Lorenzo Alberto. It was made into a film, I think, but the film was nowhere near as good as the play. The other plays on the list are: *20 Hours to Save the World*, *Youngest Child* and *24 Hours in Gower*. None of the writers is well known at all."

He paused and thought for a minute, then hastily re-read the note.

"Hang on, that's how long we're here for," said Simon. "Gosh, *24 Hours in Gower*. That's us! Has anyone got the original invitation to the funeral?"

I rustled around in my bag, pulling out empty crisp packets and discarded tampons as I hunted through. Then Julie unfolded a copy neatly from her elegant leather wallet and pushed it round the table towards Simon.

I had a pang of guilt about my own messy bag. I should have tidied it out months ago. Why couldn't I be all neat and tidy like Julie?

"YES!" said Simon. "Here we go – look – it says, 'arrive on Wednesday by 3pm, prior to the funeral on Thursday morning. You will be free to leave from 3pm on Thursday.' He wants us to be here for exactly 24 hours. Isn't that fascinating?"

"Let's have a look at the other plays: *Youngest Child*. I wonder how relevant that is?" said Mary.

"Let's find out," said Mike, leaning forward. "Is everyone here the youngest child, by any chance?"

"I'm an only child," I said.

"Me too," said Simon.

"I'm not," said Julie.

"Ah, that's that theory blown then," said Mike, sitting back in his chair. "What about the other plays you mentioned? *A Bit of a Puzzler* – what's that about? I mean – this whole thing is a bit of a puzzler."

"It's about reality and perception and what's real and what's not," said Simon. "It opens with a team of sportsmen running through a tunnel and emerging into a different world from the one they left."

"Oh God, that sounds really familiar. Really familiar. Wow – why do I know that story? I must have seen it or something but I don't really go to the theatre. How come I know it?" said Mike.

"It was made into a film," said Simon.

"Ah, that must be it," said Mike. "What was the other play on your list?"

"It was called *20 Hours to Save the World*," said Simon… Which is how much time we've been given to solve this puzzle. All those plays do seem to have a relationship to what's happening here today, except the one called *Youngest Child*. We should come back to that later."

"Do you think he was an actor who starred in them or something?" I suggested.

"Could be, but if he was a famous actor, surely there would be some sort of mention of him on Google?"

"Why don't you ring your dad and ask him whether he was involved in any of these plays, and does he know the writers behind them?" I said.

"He's dead," said Simon, bluntly. "And Mum is 96, so she doesn't have the best memory. I'll ask her though. She surprises me sometimes and seems to be able to remember things from years ago but can't remember that I went to see her yesterday. Shall we continue to go round the table first and see what everyone's got, then we can all ring our relatives based on all the joint knowledge, and see if we can come up with a picture of who this guy was."

As we spoke, bowls of miserable soup were delivered – very salty and watery. It wasn't nice at all, and most people left it. When the waitress came to clear away our plates, she looked surprised.

"No one likes it?" she said. "This soup is called the Pride of Gower Farm Hotel – it was developed in the war to feed farm helpers, and is unchanged since. All the produce in the soup was grown on Gower Farm." The bowls were taken away and our pudding was brought to the table. It was bread-and-butter pudding in chipped, mismatched bowls. It didn't bother me that the bowls didn't match each other, there was something quaint and authentic about it, but I did baulk a bit at the chips. It seemed odd that they would serve food in tatty bowls like that.

The bread-and-butter pudding was as unsophisticated as the bowls. The top was lovely and crunchy but devoid of any taste, and nowhere near enough sugar. When my mum made it, it glistened with sugar and was a real taste sensation. Underneath the crispy exterior Mum's pudding was always really soft and fluffy and warm and gooey and gorgeous. This wasn't. It had a crispiness all the way through which dug into my mouth as I ate it. The currants tasted burnt which is one of the worst tastes in the world, and its lack of sugar made it quite unpalatable. Even for someone desperately hungry after being served nothing but a bowl of soup, I struggled to eat it. As I looked around, I saw that most of the others were equally astounded by the food they had been presented with.

"We can offer you ice cream instead," said Gladys, coming in with the waitress and seeing that we'd all left it.

"Yes, please," I said, and she returned minutes later with big bowls of ice cream for us all. It looked good but I didn't hold out much hope that it would taste nice…nothing else did.

"These are called bacio ice creams," she explained. "It's

Italian for 'kiss' because it's a kiss of two flavours together and was first developed on Gower Farm."

Oh my God it was completely lovely. I couldn't believe how delicious it tasted. A silence had descended on the table. The soup was horrible, the bread rolls were stale and the bread-and-butter pudding was criminal. But this? This is was incredible. I'd never tasted such delicious ice cream before.

"Well, that was most pleasant," said Simon. "But we should move on with our investigations. Shall we talk to you, Sally? And Julie – you as well. What can you tell us? And what do your cuttings say? Sally, do you want to go first?"

"Well, I'm a teacher and I work at a school in Ascot. I've got two children and I work at a local school, I've worked there for 20 years. I've no idea why I'm here today."

"OK, what's your cutting?"

"Well, it's from 1976 and it's a piece from a newspaper about the number of nurses working in the Bristol area. The only connection I can think is that my mum was a nurse. She lives in Ascot. I know she originally worked in the Coventry area in the Midlands, but I don't know whether she ever worked in Bristol. I'll phone her and find out."

"Thank you, Sally," said Simon. "The nurse thing is interesting – the only cutting we have had that isn't related to the theatre."

"Unless he was hinting at a surgeon's theatre earlier?" I offered. "Perhaps all the theatre stuff is referring to a hospital?"

"Perhaps," said Simon. "We shouldn't rule out anything. Julie – would you like to go next?"

"Well, I work for *Marie Claire* magazine and I live in Putney, right by the river, spend most of my time socialising in Chelsea. I have done some fairly high-profile things because of being a magazine boss, but I don't know who Reginald was, and – frankly – I'm losing all interest in trying to establish his identity. This is a ludicrous waste of time. I bet there's no money to inherit at the end of it."

"I understand your frustration," said Simon, gently. "I think we're all a bit baffled by this, but if we could get all this information together it might really help us to work out what's going on. Let me clarify – did you say you were the editor of *Marie Claire* magazine?"

"More or less," replied Julie.

"You are not," said Sally. "You work in marketing there. Why do you always have to pretend you're the editor when plainly you aren't?"

"I make lots of editorial as well as marketing decisions. Stop being so petty," she said to her sister.

"OK. Look, could you just run through what your cutting is."

"Yes, as Sally said, our mother was a nurse and this cutting is about nurses. It's a piece about how kind nurses are, and how thoroughly decent they are. It doesn't have a date printed on it, but someone has scribbled 1976 on the top of it and it was in the *Bristol Post*."

"OK, so, we've definitely got an issue with the Bristol area and the theatre, and now a nurse. Julie and Sally could one of you ring your mum and ask her whether she ever worked in Bristol, and if so, when that was? Might also be useful to ask her whether she ever went to the theatre while she was in Bristol, or knew an actor called Reginald or a writing tutor called Andrew."

As Sally made notes in her small silver book, and Julie peered at herself in a small hand mirror, the door between the kitchen and the dining room opened and a tale, pale man walked in.

"Sorry to interrupt," he said. "My name is Ivor Deg, I'm from the funeral home where Mr Charters is currently resting. Would any of you like to see the body?"

"Good God, no," said Simon.

The funeral director looked surprised. He clearly had no idea of the peculiar arrangements that had found us gathered in the room.

"Would anyone like to?" he tried. "It can be nice to see the body to get closure and to see your loved one at peace. I find dead bodies quite reassuring, to be honest."

There were lots of shaking heads and people looking as if they would rather be anywhere else on earth.

"Is Mary here?" he asked.

I raised my hand tentatively, I had my wits about me this time, I wasn't going to be trapped into any more ridiculous tasks.

"Hello, Mary, are you the deceased's wife?"

"No," I said. "I've never met him."

"Oh, I thought you were giving the address at the service tomorrow."

"Yes, I am," I said.

"Right. But if you don't know him, would it not be better if someone else gave the address?"

"Absolutely. I'd be all in favour of that," I said.

"None of us knows him," said Simon, and we all clocked the look of bewilderment on Mr Deg's face.

"Sorry," he said. "How can none of you know him? I thought the gentleman wanted you all at his funeral."

"That's right," said Simon. "He did, but right now, none of us has any clue why."

Chapter 13

1954

"I DON'T UNDERSTAND WHAT I'M DOING WRONG," SAID Madelyn as she paced around the small cottage, rocking baby Joe in her arms. "He won't stop crying, whatever I do it's the same. I've fed him, changed his nappy, and winded him. Why won't he stop crying for just one minute?"

"Don't worry, dear, you're not doing anything wrong," said Marco's mum, Anna. "Just relax and let him cry if he needs to. Sing to him and cuddle him."

Anna spoke to her so kindly and gently, and had been very supportive to them both since she'd had the baby, but Madelyn felt heartbroken that her own parents couldn't be there, supporting her. They had died in a car crash two years ago, and she missed them desperately, especially now she was a mother. She'd always assumed she'd take to motherhood so easily, but it had been hard. She felt exhausted and useless.

Her brothers: Keith and Ken came over whenever they could, but they had families of their own, and were so busy on the farm, that she knew it was hard for them to stay for any length of time.

"Madelyn, don't look so worried," said Anna. "He's just a grizzly baby – some of them are born that way. He'll soon grow out of it, you'll see."

Marco's parents, Joe and Anna, had come to live with them after the baby was born, and it had been lovely to have them there to cook and care for her while Marco continued to focus on the ice cream parlour. They'd set up in the High Street after Tom and Irene had moved to North Wales, and called the place Joe's Ice Cream Parlour, after their son, and Marco's dad and grandfather.

But sometimes their flat above the shop in the High Street felt packed and noisy with so many people in it. She genuinely loved her parents in law but sometimes she wanted to scream. There was never any peace and quiet. The bell rang every time anyone went in or out of the ice cream shop below, and she would hear them talking on the street outside as they gathered in the evenings.

Madelyn hated to moan, and she knew she was lucky that Anna did so much to help out but sometimes she longed for the freedom and lightness of the life they'd enjoyed when they first got married and would spend so much time together - just the two of them, curled up around each other on the sofa, going for long walks. No stress, an easy, simple life. She felt weighed down by everything now, and felt it particularly when baby Joe was being so unbearable.

"Shall I take him for a few minutes," said Anna, seeing how low this was making her daughter-in-law feel. "You go and lie down or have a nice bath."

"Are you sure?"

"Positive," said Anna.

Madelyn handed the crying baby to Anna and walked slowly towards her bedroom, yearning for a lie down. She'd got halfway down the corridor before she realised that Joe had stopped crying. She was pleased, of course, but also overcome with disappointment and anxiety at her own abilities as a mother. Why had he stopped screaming in Anna's arms when he wouldn't stop screaming for her?

She lay on the bed and cried herself to sleep.

BY THE TIME JOE WAS FOUR YEARS OLD, MARCO AND MADELYN realised they were dealing with a child who was quite unlike the other children in the area. The incessant crying had stopped, of course, but Joe had no interest at all in being outside playing. All Joe wanted to do was read books and draw.

Joe had a very delicate disposition, hated to get dirty and didn't enjoy playing with the boys at school anywhere near as much as he enjoyed playing with the girls. He was an extraordinarily slim boy who was fussy about what he ate and would only consume the tiniest portions.

The only thing that really interested him was stories, and his parents were forced to read to him time and time again. Marco would read *Call of the Wild* to him – the novel that his father had given to him when he was little, and that he had read to Tom Junior when he was working on the farm. It was lovely that he was now regaling his son with the adventures of Squadron Leader Reginald Charters, as he had once regaled that lovely Welsh boy.

. . .

THROUGH HIS CHILDHOOD AND TEENS JOE REMAINED uninterested in the life that Madelyn and Marco lived. He said he hated business and hated farming. He became a vegetarian when he realised where meat came from, and wrote poems and songs about humanity's cruelty. He thought ice cream was disgusting and wanted nothing to do with the popular ice cream parlours that bore his name.

His great interest was in the arts and he displayed an extraordinary talent for learning poetry off by heart and reading every book he could get his hands on.

While other boys in the area went out and played rugby at the weekends, and trained in the evenings, dreaming of a red jersey and the chance to play for Wales, Joe became obsessed with Dylan Thomas. He became editor of the school news-paper and his teachers spoke of his writing talent, and how clever he was with words. When he joined his school sixth form he became chairman of the Dylan Thomas Society and instead of watching rugby matches on a Saturday, he saved up to watch plays. The thing he loved more than anything was to write: poetry, short stories and plays. Mainly plays: the theatre meant everything to him.

Marco would encourage his son to join the men for nights out, and to come to local rugby games and support his friends, but Joe had no interest. As he got older, he became more entrenched in his ways and clearer about what he wanted and who he was.

"I love that boy to death, but he's nothing like me at all," Marco would say, urging Madelyn to double-check whether she might have come home from hospital with the wrong baby.

"Ah, leave him alone. He's bright and artistic, you should be proud of him. And he's a lovely writer."

"Oh, I'm proud," said Marco. "Just a bit confused."

Marco tried going to events with his son, but it was all so other-worldly. He didn't understand the people or the excitement of watching a play that had the same outcome every time. He went to watch a series of Oscar Wilde plays with Joe but simply didn't get why his son loved them so much.

"How can you watch these plays over and over again?" his dad had said as they sat in their seats once the lights had come up.

"How can you watch sport over and over again?" Joe had countered.

"To find out what will happen. The beauty of sport is that you don't know what will happen."

"Yes you do – a bunch of rough and artless men will charge around kicking one another. They are just thugs."

"Thugs? Joe, that's ridiculous, you can't write all sports people off as thugs. And what about Oscar Wilde? He's more disgusting than all sports people put together – sleeping with other men, disgracing his family. It's vile and unnatural."

"Why does it matter what he does in his own time?" said Joe. "He's a brilliant writer – can't you just enjoy his talents?"

"Not really," said Marco. "Not knowing what he does. I can't believe they legalised it. Homosexuals are disgusting. Did you see what happened to that gay guy who ended up in hospital last week? Doctors operated on him without any anaesthetic. I don't blame them, son. It's disgusting, that's what it is – disgusting."

"So no one who's gay can do anything of merit? They will always be judged because they are gay?"

"Yes," said Marco. "Now can we go? I've had enough of this theatre to last a lifetime."

Chapter 14

1973

Joe Stilliano stood in the street and looked up at the beautiful Wills Memorial Building in the centre of Bristol. "This is amazing," he said. "It's a dream come true."

The quiet, shy boy who'd never been out of Wales stood in front of the grand university buildings and felt like he'd found his place. He couldn't believe it. He would be studying creative writing at Bristol University for the next three years – it was a dream come true. He'd studied all of the brochures from universities around the country, and this was the only one with a proper, specialist playwriting department. It was the only course that included a full term of playwriting in it. It was perfect. It was everything he'd ever wanted.

He looked at his mother whose anxiety was painted across her face. Her only son was leaving home; fear and sadness consumed her. While Madelyn fretted, Marco looked on impassively. He didn't understand why his son wanted to go to university. Not really. No one in the family had been in higher education before, and they'd all done OK for themselves. They had a nice life, didn't they? They had a thriving business in Wales with Joe's Ice Cream Parlours in Swansea, Llanelli and Carmarthen now. Each shop needed a manager and staff. He'd assumed that's what Joe would do. Enter the family business and help to build it even further.

"Listen, Mum and Dad, I know you don't really understand me," Joe said. "I know you think I should stay at home and build a life there, but I'm so happy to be here. I'm so delighted to be studying creative writing – you know how much that means to me. I want to make a mark in the world as a writer. I promise I'll make you proud."

"Oh son, we're already proud, you know that, don't you? Your father and I couldn't possibly be prouder of you. All we want is for you to be happy."

Joe smiled at his dad and hugged his mum but deep down he suspected that his dad wasn't terribly proud of him at all, because he was doing something that his dad simply didn't understand.

"All I've ever wanted for you is happiness," his mum repeated. "Be kind and be good and be happy. That's all. Can you do that?"

"I can do that," said Joe, as he kissed his mum and dad goodbye and headed off to find his room. He clutched a suitcase containing all his possessions, and on his face was a smile as wide as the ocean. Marco and Madelyn turned and walked away, hand-in-hand, sad but relieved that their only son was happy.

Chapter 15

Joe's first week at university flew past in a blur of new faces and new activities. Life was busy, challenging and fulfilling. He rang his mum and dad to tell them how much he was enjoying himself and regaled them with tales of the stories he'd written and the opportunities on offer.

"Have you made lots of friends?" asked Mum.

"Of course," he replied, even though that wasn't strictly true. But it was fine. He was happy – he didn't want friends really, they just got in the way of his studies. And it was studying and understanding writing that engaged and entranced him.

"I have to go now, mum," he said. "I'll call you soon, OK?"

He walked down the street and up the stone steps to the large wooden door of the lecture theatre and wandered inside, taking his place at the front of the room as he always did, opening his notebook and preparing to take notes.

He had no idea as he sat there, that his life was about to be transformed for ever.

The lecturer walked out, carrying a pile of books with his briefcase balanced on the top, struggling to reach his desk before dropping everything onto it.

"Morning, I'm Andrew," he said to Joe. "I'm today's lecturer."

"Morning," said Joe, looking up and falling instantly in love. He felt moved to the very centre of his soul. The lecturer was not beautiful but there was something captivating about him. He was a pale man with greying sandy hair and a cropped beard. At a guess he was around 50 and had sparkling blue eyes that held Joe's gaze, and a childlike smile that belied his age. There was something vulnerable but steely about him.

Other students drifted into the lecture theatre until the place was completely full, but to Joe it felt as if he and Andrew were the only people in the world. Andrew ran through his lesson about the art of storytelling, and as he spoke, Joe's love grew deeper. The knowledge, enthusiasm and sheer joy that Andrew conveyed startled and overjoyed him. He'd never known feelings like this. At school, boys had chased girls around and he'd kept his distance. He'd laughed with them when they described their conquests, but he'd not ever really understood what moved them to behave so oddly around girls, and he'd never had a girlfriend himself.

Now he understood why. He felt uplifted, excited but terrified beyond belief.

"Right, we'll leave it there for this week," said Andrew. The lesson had flown past with extraordinary speed. "But if anyone is interested in coming on a course that I'm holding next Saturday, the information is being handed out. Any questions?"

Joe sat, staring at Andrew from the front of the room, watching him tidy away his things before standing up to leave. Long after Andrew had walked out of the door, Joe rose slowly to his feet, packed up his things and left the building. He'd only been in there for an hour... Nothing had changed really, and yet everything had changed.

The leaflet about the playwriting course was neatly folded and tucked inside his diary. Over the next ten days he would battle with himself about whether he should go, sick with anger that he was attracted to Andrew and remembering his father's words about disgusting gays and how vile and horrendous they were; how they'd be beaten by police and abused in hospitals. He knew how much gay men were despised by society. He remembered his father's friend – the local PC Arthur Peters – talking at length about what he would do if he arrested a gay man. "I could use him for target practice," he told dad, as they drank their beers and laughed together. Marco had instilled in Joe the belief that gays were bad and they deserved bad things to happen to them. Did that make Joe bad? He didn't feel it. All he knew was that every time he thought of Andrew, the world seemed in every way brighter, warmer and happier.

TEN DAYS LATER JOE WALKED INTO THE BRISTOL PLAYHOUSE where Andrew was running the playwriting course. To the extent that he knew anything about matters of a sartorial nature, he had dressed up and was looking the best he could. He wanted to make an impression on the man who had dominated his thoughts. He had tried to convince himself that this playwriting course would help with his degree and that's why he needed to go. But that wasn't true, and he knew deep down that his presence on the course was entirely because he found Andrew so attractive.

Joe took his place at the front of the small room 10 minutes before the lecture started and pulled out his notebook. When Andrew came in, Joe's face lit up.

"We've met before, haven't we?" asked Andrew, shaking Joe's hand and sitting on the edge of his desk.

"I'm in your writing class at uni," said Joe. "It's lovely to meet you properly."

"You too," said Andrew.

There were probably around 30 years between the two men, but they looked at one another and became locked in a spell of desire.

Other people came in and took their seats, but Andrew didn't move from his position, perched on the edge of Joe's desk. Only when it was time to start did he make his way to the front, offering Joe a secret glance before leaving.

The morning passed quickly. Not only was Andrew adorable, but he was interesting; bright, informative and help-ful. And when they broke for lunch, Joe decided to do some-thing he'd never done before…to make a move. He walked up to Andrew, offered him a most dazzling smile and asked him whether he fancied lunch.

Joe had always been shy, and found it difficult to make friends and get to know people properly, but this felt different, natural. He was compelled and dazzled by Andrew – drawn to him as he'd never been drawn to anyone before. Over lunch they chatted about everything…their backgrounds, their ambi-tions, the things they loved and the things they hated.

"How many relationships have you had?" asked Andrew.

"None," said Joe, shyly. He didn't feel the need to lie. "I never chased girls when I was younger, and I never hung around with the guys who went out looking for girls. It never appealed to me. I didn't see the point. I had lots of girl 'friends' but not girlfriends. I've never been in love. How about you?"

"I had girlfriends when I was younger. I went out with them largely because it was the thing to do. I don't think I ever thought about the fact that I might not actually be attracted to them, or indeed to any girls. I didn't admit the truth to myself for years."

"The truth?"

"That I am gay. I'm attracted to men. It's who I am, there's nothing I can do about it. When I was your age it was illegal to be gay so it's not been easy. Nothing's easy when you're attracted to men. How long have you known you were gay?"

"Um, I didn't really know I was gay. I don't know that I am. I mean – I just don't know."

Andrew looked up and checked that no one was watching them, before he reached over and kissed Joe on the lips.

"How was that?" he asked.

"Lovely," Joe replied, honestly.

"You're gay," he said. "Would you like to come out on a date with me?"

"Yes. I'd love to," Joe said without hesitation. He felt a light flutter run through him, the sort of flutter of a million songs and poems, the sort of flutter he had never known. He was tapping into experiences today that were totally new. He went home that evening to his small room in the halls of residence and wrote the date in his notebook: 29 September 1973. The date when everything changed. The date he'd met Andrew.

The date he'd fallen in love. The date that would set in motion a catalogue of events that would ruin his life, but through the years, when Joe looked back, he knew he wouldn't change anything, nothing at all, about that date, that moment, and his feelings for that man.

Chapter 16

1976

JOE STOOD IN FRONT OF THE MIRROR AND SIGHED. HE DIDN'T
know what the meeting today with Andrew would bring.
They'd not seen each other all summer. Joe had been with his
mother in Wales, nursing Madelyn through her final weeks.
The cancer had taken every part of her: it had stopped her
physically, slowed her movement and eventually closed down
her breathing. But she'd remained bright and warm until the
bitter end. She'd smiled when she could, looking at her son so
lovingly as he gently stroked her hand.

"I've had a good life," she'd said. "A good life because I
met your father – what a great man he was – and because of
you. He loved you so much, Joe. He thought the world of
you."

"And I of him," Joe had said, gently stroking his mother's

hand. There were so many times when he wanted to tell her that he had met someone and was in love. He thought she might be reassured to hear that he had someone to look after him when she was gone. But what if it just worried her more? What if she had no idea he was gay and went to her death fearful of what the future would hold. So he stroked her hand, and talked about the past, and didn't mention Andrew or what sort of future he would have without her. On what would turn out to be her last day he'd arrived to find her lying on the bed looking so hauntingly fragile that he wanted to sweep her into his arms and protect her forever. Her eyes were barely open, and wisps of hair stuck up from her head. She'd always been such an attractive woman. His friends at school had always told him what a beautiful mother he had. Always well-groomed despite the long hours spent working in the ice cream parlours.

"Joe, brush my hair for me, would you? Make me look nice for when I meet your father again."

Joe choked back the tears as he brushed his mother's soft, thinning hair. Her luxurious mane had been destroyed by age and cancer treatments. As he brushed, his mother closed her eyes, a gentle smile came to rest on her lips and quietly she'd drifted away.

He'd organised the funeral, knowing it would be well attended. His mother and father were such popular people. Joe had asked Andrew to come with him on this visit home because he knew it would be the last time he would see his mother, and he wanted Madelyn to meet Andrew. Joe wouldn't tell her that they were lovers if he were there; just that they were friends.

But Andrew felt uncomfortable about it. He thought it would cause too much gossip locally, and that wasn't right.

He'd said that having never met Madelyn it was better all-round if he didn't come.

Joe had agreed, reluctantly, that this was a sensible solution, but somewhere deep down inside him he felt hurt by Andrew's actions. He was worried that Andrew was pulling away from him and the thought of losing the love of his life at the same time as he lost his mum was unbearable. While he was in Wales, burying his mum, he yearned to have reassurance from Andrew that everything was OK. Joe wrote to him daily, begging him to come, urging him to call and let him know that all was well. In the manner of a million jilted lovers, his desperation for reassurance drove the object of his affections further away.

JOE STRUGGLED TO UNDERSTAND WHAT HAD GONE WRONG after three years of dating. It had been so wonderful to start with... after meeting on the course, they had gone on long walks in the countryside and sneakily held hands when they were out of sight, enjoying picnics by the river and late-night talks. Joe had felt whole, he'd felt alive and vibrant and as if he were walking on a ground made of the softest clouds. Everything he experienced felt like it had come straight from the cheesiest pop songs. Now he understood why great works of art, great poems and the most popular songs were invariably about love.

Joe found himself feeling free and lighter than he had since he was a young boy. He knew what his role in life was – it was to be with Andrew, supporting and helping him. He knew that clearly. Everything made sense now. He was growing intellectually under Andrew's guidance. It didn't matter that Andrew was much older, in fact it made it better.

Joe had been unsure of the world and nervous about the relationship he was embarking upon, so having someone there who was worldly, sophisticated and experienced had made it much easier. Life had been joyful and Joe had thought it would last forever.

He couldn't quite put his finger on the moment when things changed. It wasn't anything in particular…no one thing happened that changed their relationship or created a tension between them that wasn't there before. Joe simply started to feel as if Andrew wasn't as bothered about coming to see him. Andrew had stopped trying, and no matter that Joe tried twice as hard, hard enough for both of them he thought, it still didn't work. Andrew barely acknowledged him at the graduation ceremony when Joe was awarded his first-class honours degree with a distinction for play writing. When they did see one another, Andrew no longer made any effort. The romance had gone and the passion was gone.

Now Joe was back in Bristol, preparing for the next stage of his education – an MA in play writing. He looked at himself in the mirror, tonight he would see Andrew after their summer apart. He'd bought a new shirt, but as he stood there with the stiff material tucked into his new jeans, it looked all wrong. It was too formal. He looked miserable…the whole thing wasn't him at all.

He desperately wanted to look good when he saw Andrew. He ached with desire to see the man he loved, and he wanted to make the best possible impression. But at the same time, he feared an evening of stilted conversation and awkward moments. He feared most of all that he would be dumped. But still he would go, he would meet Andrew while looking the best he could, and he would hope against hope that everything would somehow, miraculously, be OK.

Joe walked out of the small apartment he was renting next to the university and headed into the chilly autumn evening.

The harsh steps towards winter had begun: flowers no longer sat in the gardens and the warm expectant air of summer had been replaced with a biting chill. He wished he'd brought his jacket. And some gloves. He rubbed his hands together and blew into them, speeding up his walk towards the park and to the small pub on the other side where he and Andrew had arranged to meet.

As he strode along the pavement, kicking leaves underfoot, his mind was so focused on the meeting ahead of him that he hardly saw the man walking towards him until the guy was in front of him and had blocked his way.

"Going somewhere?" the stranger asked.

"Yes," said Joe, moving to step round the young man in a black leather jacket. He wasn't a big man but had a menacing air.

"Going to meet your boyfriend?" he asked.

Joe became vaguely aware of other men gathering to the side. He felt fear rise up inside him. They had obviously been watching him and Andrew. Joe was used to rude comments being shouted out at him, of course, but nothing like this. No one had made him feel quite this scared.

"Cat got your tongue?" It wasn't the guy in the leather jacket this time, it was one of the others. Joe turned to look and as he did, he felt a crushing blow to the side of his head.

"Faggot," came the shout. "Bloody faggot. Joe Stilliano, you're a fucking faggot. Yeah, don't look so shocked – we know your name, gay boy."

A kick to his groin left him doubled over in pain.

"Fucking bummer."

Smack.

"Pervert."

Whack.

He crumbled to the ground while kicks and insults rained down on him. He prayed he would live through it, and prayed, more than anything, that they would not go after Andrew. Let them beat me enough for both of us, he thought.

"Fucking homo."

Kick.

"Christ. Is he dead?"

BLACKNESS.

Chapter 17

2018

IVOR DEG, THE FUNERAL DIRECTOR, COULD NOT GET OUT OF the room fast enough once he realised that none of the people going to the funeral knew who Reginald Charters was. It was quite the most ridiculous thing he'd ever heard. Why were they going if they didn't know him? And where were this Reginald chap's real friends? He smiled a half smile and backed towards the door. Then he remembered.

"Oooh, I have this," he said, dropping a large envelope on the table. "I was told to give it to you. Have a good evening. See you tomorrow."

Simon picked up the envelope and read the writing on the front.

This is an envelope containing the notes for Tom Gower who should be here with you today, but who Reginald was unable to track down.

"We'll look in this later, shall we? When we've been through everyone who's here," said Simon. "Now, where were we? Um – Mike, do you want to run through a little bit about yourself, and what cutting you've been given?"

"Sure, OK. Well I am a TV executive at SKY, I live in Twickenham and I'm obsessed with rugby, as you can probably see from the size of me."

He delivered this line with a slight raise of his eyebrows and a gentle look over to where Julie was sitting, staring at him with undisguised lust. In all honesty Mike wasn't that big, and I wouldn't have had him down as a rugby player, but it didn't surprise me at all that he worked at SKY. He looked exactly like one of their absolutely perfect, white-toothed presenters.

"My cutting makes sense to me. It's a mock-up of an advert for a bed and breakfast in Bristol. It's got a picture of a green B&B over a map of Bristol. My dad, who is now dead, ran a bed and breakfast in Bristol for years. It's funny because it was the same gaudy green colour as in the picture. I remember my mum would nag Dad about the horrible colour all the time.

"She'd say to him 'Do you know – people navigate their way around this area of Bristol using our business to guide them. They say "go to the disgusting green B&B and turn left at the roundabout". Do we really want people talking about our place like that? Using its ugliness as a local landmark? Why don't we paint it a lovely, elegant cream colour and have colourful window boxes. It would look so much better.'

"But my dad insisted that the fact that it stood out, and people used it in their directions around the area meant that everyone knew where it was. 'It's good for business, Sarah' he would insist. 'The first thing you need to do as a business owner is make sure that people know where you are. Well, everyone knows where we are. It's perfect.'"

So, Mike explained how the B&B had retained its reptilian colour as a result and now here it was again, in front of him.

"Obviously I can't ask Dad whether he's ever heard of Reginald Charters, but I will call my mum and see what she says. I asked her whether she'd heard of him when I got the invitation and she said she hadn't, but – you never know – I'll try again."

Simon scribbled down notes as Mike spoke.

"Yes – do ask your mum if she can add anything to the story. Any information would be useful. Now, last but not least, Mr Matt Prior, do you want to tell us a little bit about yourself?"

Matt turned a rather alarming shade of scarlet. "Yes, my name is Matthew but everyone calls me Matt, I'm 19 and I'm on a carpentry apprenticeship," he said in a soft Welsh accent. "I live just outside Cardiff with my mum and dad, and I don't know who Reginald Charters was. My clue is very strange. It's a taxi receipt from 1976 with a smiling emoji along with a cross, like a medical cross, I guess. That's all I have."

"Ah, a medical cross? I wonder whether that relates to Julie and Sally's mum. Is your dad a taxi driver?" asked Simon.

"No," said Matt. "He's a carpenter."

"OK," said Simon. "Could you ring your dad and ask him whether anyone in the family would have been a taxi driver in 1976, and if so which area?"

"Yes, sure," said Matt. "I'll ask him."

"Right," said Simon. "This is all giving me a huge headache, but I do think we found some similarities and possible links to the family members. Certainly, we know that the key dates are between 1973 and 1976. Shall we have a break, and ring around relatives to see what they can tell us?"

"Shouldn't we look at the envelope that spooky-looking guy gave us?" said Sally. "You never know – it might help."

"Oh yes, of course, I'd forgotten about that."

Simon carefully opened the manila envelope and pulled out some notes.

"Oh," he said. "That's not very helpful. It's a cutting from 1943 when a load of Italian prisoners of war came over to Wales to be based on farms, helping farmers til the end of the war."

"So, do you think he was a prisoner of war?" asked Matt. "I remember learning about them at school."

"He couldn't have been," said Simon. "He wasn't born until – hang on – um, around 1950ish."

"Perhaps his dad came over as a prisoner of war?"

"That's a real possibility." Simon squinted as he did the basic maths in his head and calculated that – yes – the dates worked out. "But why would an Italian call his son Reginald?"

"So that he assimilated? So he seemed like a local?" suggested Mike.

"Could be," said Simon, nodding his head. "Let's all go and make our phone calls and have a little break and come back to this feeling a bit fresher."

There were murmurs of approval, largely at the suggestion of a break, but also because we knew we had to talk to our relatives in order to make sense of everything. There was a million pounds at stake, everyone wanted to work this out.

"I'll see whether we can get some drinks, shall I?" said Simon, looking around the table.

"Yes please," I said. "If there are any snacks or anything, that would be great. Lunch wasn't all that wonderful, was it?"

"No, indeed," said Simon. "You never got your egg and cress after all, did you?" He smiled warmly at me and ruffled my hair and I decided I really liked him.

"Let's meet back here in an hour, shall we? Six o'clock?"

Chapter 18

I walked back up to my room, sat on the small chair which creaked alarmingly beneath my weight, so I eased myself of it gently, and went to lie down on the bed. I scanned through all the notes I had. Although I knew Mum didn't have a clue who Reginald Charters was, and I didn't feel I had any new information to impart, I thought I ought to make an effort and ring her

"Mum, I'm here, in Wales preparing for this funeral tomorrow."

"Oh how exciting, tell me – who was this guy?"

"Well, that's the thing – we still don't know, Mum, he gave us some clues, but didn't tell us who he was, he wanted us to guess. We should find out for definite after the funeral tomorrow, but we're trying to work it out because he said we'd inherit his money if we worked it out. It's really strange. I've got a bit more information. Can you have a think about this, and work out whether you know anyone who fits this bill?"

I went through everything with Mum, the dates, the relevant places, and exactly what we were trying to find out. She shouted out to my dad in the background, but I could hear him saying he hadn't got a clue, and that I was to make sure I was OK.

"Sorry, love, neither of us knows who this guy could be. The name doesn't ring a bell at all with me, or your dad, I've rung everywhere I can think of and we just don't know him."

"OK, Mum, but make sure you let me know if you think of anything at all, won't you?"

"Of course I will. You look after yourself. Your father will pick you up at the station when you come back tomorrow."

"Thanks," I said. I didn't really want to stay in the room by myself, and was hoping that if I went for a wander around and about, I might see some snacks somewhere, so I headed back down. I peeked into the rooms downstairs, but they were all just drawing rooms and libraries with big white sheets thrown over the armchairs like something out of the Victorian era, so I went back to the room we'd been sitting to find Matt, Mike and Sally still there. There was no sign of Julie.

"Hello, do you mind if I join you?" I asked.

"Of course not," said Sally. "Have you had any luck unearthing any more information?"

"Not a thing," I confessed. "Mum doesn't even recognise the name, and we're not an arty sort of family so we're certainly not the sort of people who go on theatre writing courses or anything like that. I just don't know why I'm here. I wish I could help. It would be great to solve this puzzle."

"It's the oddest thing I've ever known," said Matt. "And this house feels haunted to me – don't you think? Everything creaks and the whole place makes me feel uncomfortable. I'm sure my jacket moved off my chair onto my bed, I definitely didn't leave it on my bed."

"You probably did but just forgot about it," said Sally. "Clothes don't move themselves. And any way if there were a ghost…"

Sally was halfway through her sentence when all the lights in the room went out, plunging us into complete darkness. It wasn't like at home where the light from other rooms seeped in, or the lights of other houses offered some brightness, this was total blackness.

"Christ," said Matt. "I told you this place was haunted."

"Just relax," said Sally. "They'll come back on in a minute. Try not to panic."

"OK," said Matt's shaky voice. "We're here because a dead man we've never met invited us and now all the lights have gone out, but I'll try not to panic."

"It's probably just the electricity short circuiting," said Sally. "I'm sure someone will be down soon to fix it."

We sat in silence again. I rather hoped Mike might offer to go and investigate but he sat there, not saying a word. My Ted would have jumped up to find out what was going on. And so would Simon. Simon? Where was Simon?

We sat in silence a little longer, then things got really scary as a howl came from outside. "Oh Christ alive," said Matt. "We're all going to die. I knew I shouldn't have come. I just knew it."

Next there was a creek and the sound of movement outside, followed by the slamming of a car door.

"It's Reginald's ghost come to haunt us," said Matt.

"What? In a car?" said Sally, dismissively. "Do ghosts really drive cars?"

Then footsteps…slowly crunching through the gravel. I felt terrified, thinking this could actually be where we all got shot.

The door eased open with a haunting squeak. I didn't want

to die. I dived under the table and I felt Matt drop down next to me. Then the lights came on.

"Hi, everyone," said Simon. "What are you doing sitting in the dark?"

I slowly edged myself back into my chair.

"And what are you doing on the floor? Are you playing some sort of game? I haven't spoilt your fun, have I?"

"My God, man, you terrified us," said Matt. "I thought you were Reginald's ghost come to haunt us."

"I went to the shop." He smiled and held up two carrier bags. "Mary said she was hungry and I thought we could all do with a snack, so I nipped out while you were in your rooms and thought I'd surprise you with this little lot. Didn't expect to come back to find you all sitting in the pitch black."

There was a loud thud as he plonked down the two bags, and we all looked at each other, embarrassed. Then the door opened and Julie walked in. "Sorry, darlings, I didn't plunge you into darkness, did I? I was trying to find the outside lights and I think I turned all the house lights off, I put them back on again as soon as I realised what I'd done but they're all bloody complaining out there in reception."

"No problem at all," said Matt. "We all thought it was something like that."

Chapter 19

1976

THE CROWD OF MEN WHO BEAT UP JOE STILLIANO HADN'T MEANT
to leave him lying on the ground, begging for his life. As they
raced away from him, to a man they felt that they had over-
done things. One guy glanced back, terrified of what they
might have done. They'd beaten this guy so badly that he lay
in a pool of blood, his breathing shallow, clearly in pain. The
deal had been that they would teach him a lesson after he'd
been seen poncing around with that other gay guy – the older
one. But then they hadn't seen him out and about all summer
and when they'd knocked on the door of the flat they'd
believed to be his, there'd been no answer. For weeks they'd
waited for him but he hadn't appeared. Then, when they saw
him, they reacted – quickly and brutally.

A guy in an old denim jacket wondered whether he should

go back. Or should he find a phone box and ring an ambulance?

"Run, James," shouted Ed, the leader of the pack. He'd been the one to throw the first punch. He was well aware that if James hung around and got caught they would all be implicated. If the bender died, they'd be on a murder charge. He grabbed his mate by the collar of his denim jacket and pulled him so he stumbled into a run. "Fucking run."

And so, James ran. He ran as fast as he could away from the man lying in the ever-growing pool of blood.

JOE LAY STILL. SPRAWLED ACROSS THE PAVEMENT ON THE QUIET street until a taxi passed, stopped and reversed until it was alongside him.

"Are you OK, mate?" asked the driver, getting out before he saw the full extent of the injuries.

"Jesus Christ, mate. Can you hear me? Are you OK?"

Joe could hear the voice through a veil of pain. He tried to nod but couldn't manage to move anything.

"Wait here for two minutes, I'm going to get help," said the man.

Joe tried to open his eyes…everything was blurred. He closed them and listened as a car drove past, birds tweeted. It was such a quiet street. What if the man didn't come back? When would he be found? He closed his eyes and drifted off to sleep.

Minutes later he awoke to the sound of voices: a man and a woman – the same man as before, talking to him, telling Joe that his name was Fred Radex, and he would try to help him.

"What's your name?" asked a soft female voice. "My

name's Daphne and I'm a nurse." She sounded young. He guessed she was pretty. She sounded like she might be pretty.

"Joe," he said.

"Good, OK, Joe, there's nothing to worry about. We're going to help you. Can you squeeze my hand?"

Joe squeezed with all his might and heard the nurse give a little yelp.

"Well, there's nothing wrong with that squeeze," she said kindly. "I think we can safely say you're going to survive; we just need to get you to hospital. Have you called the police, Fred?"

"No!" cried Joe, as loud as his bruised ribs would allow. "Please no. No police. No hospital. I beg of you – don't call the police. Just take me back to my flat and I'll be fine."

There was no way he was going anywhere near a hospital and he would not allow them to call the police – he knew the attack would end up in the paper and the reasons for the attack would be known to everyone. He wouldn't allow that. And he remembered so clearly what his dad had said all those years ago about the way in which gay men were treated by doctors. He remembered the way people would talk about gays and the dreadful way in which they were treated. He remembered what Arthur Peters had said, the local policeman who'd described gay men as 'target training.' That wasn't going to happen to him.

"You need medical attention," said Daphne. "I can't just leave you, you're really unwell. We need to get you to a hospital."

"I'd rather die than go to hospital…you have to understand," said Joe. "Please don't take me to hospital."

He moved to sit up but his stomach hurt so much that he rolled back onto his side.

"Let's get him off the street," said Fred. "Then we can work out what to do."

"Can you walk?" they asked Joe.

He struggled to sit up again.

"Hang on," said Fred. "I'll just go and get some help."

Daphne knelt down beside Joe while the man was gone and spoke to him gently.

Did he know what year it was? What was the name of the Prime Minister? How many fingers was she holding up?

He could answer the questions but the fingers meant nothing to him. There was just a blur.

"Andrew!" he said, remembering, quite suddenly. "I'm supposed to be meeting Andrew in the bar. How long have I been here? He'll still be waiting. I need to tell him I can't come."

"You don't need to do anything," said the nurse. "You need to lie very still, then we'll get you out of here and check what damage has been done. I think you'll need to go to hospital, but let's worry about that later."

Joe could feel his heart beating faster. He didn't want to be taken anywhere except to Andrew. "He'll be cross if I leave him waiting," said Joe. "I need to talk to him."

"He won't be cross when he sees what's happened," said the nurse, wiping gently at his eyes. "Can you see my fingers now?" Joe looked out and realised he could.

"Three," he said, confidently.

"Well done. You've got lots of blood in your eyes. Once we've cleaned you up, you'll feel a hundred times better."

He saw the taxi driver return with another man.

"I'm not going to hospital and I don't want you to call the police," said Joe. "Please, promise me you won't."

"This is Nicholas Sween," said the man. "He and his wife

Sarah own the bed and breakfast just there – the funny-looking green one. We're going to take you in there and get you a drink of water, then we must get you to hospital."

"No hospital," growled Joe. "I can't go to hospital. Please don't make me."

The two men glanced at one another, wondering what the kid had against the police and doctors, then they lifted Joe onto his feet. The woman with the soft voice wiped his face again and replaced his broken glasses on his nose.

"We're not taking you to hospital. Just relax. We're going to look after you."

"No police."

"OK, no police, let's just get you off the street and work out what to do."

Joe moved quietly next to them, leaning onto the men who supported his weight on their shoulders. He was taken to the B&B and into a reception area where he heard a woman gasp and hushed voices talking. Then he was being laid down. He heard them mention hospital and he repeated his heartfelt desire not to be taken to hospital. He'd rather die than face the judgement of the authorities. He'd rather never recover from his injuries than be forced to discuss with medical staff why he had been attacked, what he'd been called and what his private life entailed.

They laid Joe down on the sofa.

"Here, I'm just going to bathe your face," said Daphne, crouching down next to him. He heard the swishing of water and then felt a warm damp flannel on his face.

"Tell me if I'm hurting you," said the nurse. "I'm just wiping away the blood so we can see what the damage is."

"Thank you," said Joe. The feeling of her cloth on his skin

was painful but he lay there and let her finish. He felt he'd moaned enough.

"I think your nose is broken," she said. "And there's a nasty cut above your eye. There's every chance your cheekbone is broken too. They'll fix you up in no time in hospital."

"No!" said Joe.

"Can you tell me why?" asked the nurse, she wiped the top of his head again with a flannel while she spoke.

"Just take me back to my flat, I'll be fine there."

"We will do no such thing. Will you tell me what's worrying you so much about the police and hospital?"

Joe struggled to open his eyes. He could see there were two of them standing there.

Daphne sensed his reluctance to speak.

"Nicholas, any chance you could put the kettle on for me and bring me some boiling water?"

When Nicholas left the room, Joe knew he had to tell the nurse the truth.

"They beat me up because I'm gay. They called me names and said they hoped I'd die."

There was a silence in the room.

"You're disgusted, aren't you?" said Joe. "You're completely disgusted with me. I do understand. I'm disgusted with myself but I can't help it...I was born this way; it wasn't my choice."

"I'm not at all disgusted," said the nurse. "And neither will the doctors at the hospital be disgusted. They will look after you whether you're gay or not."

"That's not true, and you know it. Most of them think it should still be illegal, and we all know what the police do if they get their hands on gay men."

"No one will treat you badly, you have to believe me," said the nurse, but Joe shook his head.

"A few years ago they'd have been able to throw me in jail for being gay. I've heard of lots of people like me who've ended up in police stations and hospitals and been abused and beaten half to death." Joe was gasping for breath as he spoke, he was close to tears.

"OK," said the nurse. "Calm down. Please don't worry. I'll care for you, but you must do as I say, or you'll be very ill."

"Yes, I will," said Joe. "I'll do exactly what you ask me to do."

"OK. Well – first of all, where are your parents? Your mum and dad?"

And that's when Joe broke down. He had stayed calm through his mother's last days, coping with the loss of the woman he loved more than life itself. He'd organised the funeral and avoided crying throughout it. He'd been erudite when he gave his speech. Then he'd returned to Bristol to face the certainty of being dumped by the man who'd come to mean more to him than any other man. He'd even coped with being beaten up by an angry mob. But now, as he lay there, being tended to by a kindly stranger, the whole thing got the better of him.

"My mum died, I buried her last week," he said through gasping tears. "I've lost mum and dad."

"I'm sorry," said the nurse, while Joe wailed.

"The man I've been seeing, he's much older than me. I don't think he loves me any longer. He wouldn't come to the funeral," Joe added, then he sobbed and sobbed while the lovely nurse gently held his head and allowed him to release his pain.

"Where were you due to meet this man?" asked Daphne.

"The Three Ducks, the pub through the park," said Joe.

"OK, I'll go and see him and explain what's happened. Give me your key, and I'll go and collect your things from your flat as well," said the nurse.

"Thank you so much," said Joe, laying his head back on the cushions. She placed a warm blanket over him and padded out of the room.

Chapter 20

WHEN DAPHNE WALKED INTO THE PUB IT DAWNED ON HER THAT she had no idea what Andrew looked like. She'd relied on being able to walk around, look at the men sitting on their own, and work out which of them was gay. It wasn't so easy. There were quite a few men sitting by themselves, poring over the newspapers or reading books.

She smiled at one or two of them before approaching a small blonde man with two dogs at his feet.

"Are you Andrew?" she asked. "Waiting for Joe?"

The man shook his head, but she noticed the older man at the next table look up. "Are you looking for Andrew?" he said, jumping to his feet.

"Yes, hi – I'm Daphne," she said. "I'm afraid Joe's been hurt."

Andrew looked worried. "Hurt? How? What's happened?"

She explained that he'd been set upon by a group of thugs and was at the B&B recuperating. "I'm a nurse," she said. "I'm taking care of him. He's very worried about the fact that you are here waiting for him, so I thought I'd better come and explain. Do you want to come with me to see him?"

Andrew dropped his eyes and looked down at his hands, fidgeting in his lap. "I don't know," he said.

"He's not expecting you… I just thought I should ask. Why don't you want to come?"

"Our relationship has been over for months," Andrew said. "I think it would be a huge mistake to come."

Daphne nodded. His answer was sensible if not particularly caring. She'd didn't take much to this guy, to be honest. Joe could do better. She stood up to go. "Whatever you want," she said dismissively.

"Don't call the police, will you?" said Andrew. "He'd really hate that. He's got a phobia."

"Yes, so I understand," said Daphne.

"I'm sorry," said Andrew. "He's a lovely man, but I don't love him and it would be wrong for me to rush to his bedside and pretend that I do."

Next she went to Joe's flat – a small, sparsely decorated place. It contrasted so much with her own chaotic flat which she shared with two other nurses – it was always full of noise and music and was messy all the time.

Joe's place was so cold and dismal, and he had so few things in it that she decided to pack them all up and take them to the B&B. A young man in a denim jacket, waiting outside, offered to help. He said he knew Joe and asked how he was. Daphne explained that he'd been badly beaten up and was recuperating locally.

"Will he be OK?" asked the young man.

"Eventually," said Daphne. "But he's not feeling great at the moment."

Once she had all of Joe's belongings in the car she drove

back to the B&B and unpacked everything into the room that Nicholas had earmarked.

"Blimey, how long is he staying for?" asked Sarah, helping to carry the piles of books upstairs.

"I think he'll need to stay for a couple of weeks, if that's OK," said Daphne. "There's no way he can go back to that flat on his own."

"Sure," said Sarah, glancing at Nicholas. It was tough running a Bed and Breakfast. Turning paying customers away for two weeks would be difficult. They would do it, ofcourse, but it would make life hard for them.

Chapter 21

JOE HAD SPENT A WEEK IN BED RELAXING AND WAS STARTING TO
feel much better, thanks to the kind nurse who'd come every
day to look after him. Now he needed to get up, walk around
and stretch his legs. He climbed out of bed, gingerly at first,
then walked across the room to the old wooden door, undoing
the latch and stepping onto the landing.

He walked cautiously down the stairs. Sitting halfway was
a boy, staring disconsolately at the carpet. The boy had his
head in his hands and appeared to be desperately sad.

"Are you OK?" asked Joe, making the boy jump out of his
skin.

"No, I'm not, I'm... Wow, what happened to your face?
Have you been in a fight? Did you win?"

The boy looked fascinated, more intrigued than scared by
the sight of Joe on the stairs.

"It was kind of a fight," said Joe. "But I didn't have much
of a chance, there were a lot of them and only me. I was

attacked by them in the street and I'm afraid they won. As you can see!"

"Wow," he said. "Fighting is awesome."

"This wasn't really that awesome, I can assure you," said Joe. "It was pretty terrible really. Is your dad the owner of this place?"

"Yes," said the boy.

"Well your dad was very kind and he came and helped me and he let me stay here while I get better. I've been fast asleep for days!"

"I wish my dad was kind to me," said the boy. "He hates me."

"I'm sure that's not true. My name is Joe by the way, Joe Stilliano."

"I'm Michael Sween."

"How old are you, Michael?" asked Joe.

"I'm 12."

"And why do you think your father hates you?"

"Because he forces me to do homework and I hate it. I have to write a story for English called 'A Bit of a Puzzler' – how am I supposed to do that? I hate making up stories."

"You may be in luck – I can't do many things very well, but you know what I am very good at…" said Joe.

"What?" asked Michael.

"Writing. Do you want me to help you?"

"Yes please, mister. Come up to my bedroom and I'll show you my assignment," he said.

Joe sensed that going into a young boy's bedroom was definitely not advisable.

"Why don't you and get your books from your room and meet me downstairs and we'll work on the project together? Does that sound OK?"

Michael's face lit up when he smiled. He was going to be very handsome when he grew up, with his mop of dark hair and dimpled chin. Michael raced upstairs to collect everything he needed for his project while Joe sat down at the large dining room table to wait for him.

Five minutes later, Michael came barrelling down the stairs, taking them two at a time. He threw a pile of books in front of Joe. "This is it," he said. "I've got to write a story and I've got to try and make it two whole pages long."

"Well, luckily, I can help. Now – tell me what's the biggest puzzle you can think of?"

"Well, the biggest puzzle I can think of is that Barry Angel is not in the England rugby team," said Michael. "He plays for Bristol and he's brilliant. Even my dad agrees with me. He's the best player and he should be in the team."

Joe laughed. "You like sport, do you?"

"Yes," replied Michael. "I'm going to play rugby for England one day."

"Good," said Joe. "I will definitely come and watch you play. Well if you like rugby and are going to play for England, why don't we have a story about an England rugby team for your homework?"

"Yes," said Michael, his face alight at the thought.

"It needs to be a big puzzle for the rugby team, so...why don't we write a story about a rugby team who turn up to play in a big match, but when they run through the tunnel to go onto the pitch they come out in a totally different world. That would be a puzzle, wouldn't it? How did they get there? What's going on?"

"Yes," shrieked Michael. "A world with aliens and dinosaurs in it. I want it to scare my sister."

"I didn't know you had a sister."

"Yes, she's much older than me and she's staying with grandma and grandpa this week."

"OK, well let's write a story that will scare her then. It could be a world in which all the animals and the trees can talk?"

"Yes," said Michael. "And the trees start fighting. But how do we write the story. I'm not very good at writing."

"Well, we just start at the beginning. Let's start writing about the team all arriving for the match. What shall we call the team?"

"The Sween Rovers," said Michael. "That's my name."

"What are you two up to?" said Nicholas, walking into the room. Joe jumped to his feet, suddenly worried that his kind host might be suspicious of his motives, sitting down and chatting to a young boy.

"I'm doing my homework, Dad," said Michael, his face full of excitement. "We're writing the best story ever. Joe's helping me and he's brilliant at stories."

"Thanks," said Nicholas, smiling at Joe. "Very decent of you. I'm hopeless at anything like that – not a creative bone in my body. How are you feeling?"

"I'm feeling much better. Thank you. Thanks for all you've done."

Chapter 22

IT WAS ALMOST THREE WEEKS BEFORE JOE COULD LEAVE THE B&B, and by the time he did he was feeling stronger than he had for ages. His face bore the scars of his beating and as he moved towards the front door, accompanied by Daphne, Fred, Sarah and Nicholas, he felt sore, but he no longer suffered from the extreme pain as he had in his first weeks.

As he reached the door he stopped suddenly and flinched a little at the thought of going outside. He'd been safely cocooned for so many weeks that fear ran through him at the idea of going into the big, wide, frightening and judgemental world outside.

"OK?" Daphne asked.

"Just a little overwhelmed," he replied.

"You're going to be fine," said Nicholas. "Head up. Don't let anyone judge you."

"Thank you," said Joe. "Thank you so much for everything you've done. You've been so kind, and so generous. One day I'll pay you back for your kindness. I promise."

"No need," said Sarah. "Seeing you up and about and looking so well is payment enough."

"No – I will. I promise you. I will pay you back one day, all of you. Just you wait."

Joe hugged Daphne tightly. He still felt soreness in his ribs, but he wouldn't let the shiver of pain stop him from the need to show affection to this lovely woman.

"You take care, lad," said Fred, shaking his hand. "You're a good kid. Don't let anyone tell you otherwise."

"Come on then," said Nicholas. "Let me help you with these bags."

The plan was for Fred to drive Joe to the station in his taxi, then for Joe to head on to Wales. He'd given in his notice at the flat in Bristol, and needed to get away from the place for a while. He would live in his parents' flat above the ice cream parlour for a few weeks while he worked out what to do.

His plans to do a Master's degree at Bristol University would have to wait. He didn't want to be anywhere where the thugs might find him, and he had no desire to subject himself to a course lectured by a man who he loved so deeply but who no longer loved him.

His relationship with Andrew had been wonderful for two and a half years, but for the last six months of it, it had been difficult. Andrew had stayed with him because he was going through so much…he realised that. And in many ways, he thanked Andrew for not calling it off when Joe was half way through his finals, or tending to his sick mother. Andrew was a good man, and he had transformed Joe's life and made him truly happy for the first time. But he couldn't be around him, because deep-down, despite everything, he still loved Andrew.

"You stay in touch, OK?" said Fred.

"You saved my life," replied Joe, in tears. "I swear, you saved my life. You found me and saved me."

"Your life shouldn't have been in danger in the first place, with those thugs attacking you like that. I wish you'd have let me call the police. I swear they should be behind bars."

"I'm sure that's exactly where they'll end up," said Joe. "Thanks so much."

The two men hugged and Joe climbed out of the taxi, waving goodbye before heading to the platform.

Fred turned the taxi round, and waved at Joe in the rear-view mirror.

Joe waved back without turning around. He was terrified and hated being away from the security of the B&B and the nurturing attentions of Daphne.

Chapter 23

THE SMALL FLAT ON THE HIGH STREET IN LLANELLI WAS exactly as Joe remembered it from when he was a little boy. The family had lived there until he was around 13, then they had moved out and bought a nice house in the countryside when his grandparents had died, and left them the money to buy a bigger place, but they had always kept the small flat. As Joe walked in, he was transported straight back to his child-hood. The place was an arrow through time, linking the Joe of today with the small, shy boy of yesteryear. He settled down in the armchair and thought about himself as a little boy in the flat, refusing to come down to the ice cream parlour for his birthday party and hiding under the table so his dad couldn't find him. Nothing much had changed in the intervening years. OK, maybe he didn't hide under the table anymore, but age and a good education had done nothing to erase the fear of socialising that ran through his veins. He'd been so unlike his sociable parents…always wanting to hide away and not see anyone. He kicked off his shoes, dropped his head to one side and nodded off to sleep.

When Joe woke hours later to sounds on the street down below, he sat up with a start. He'd forgotten how noisy it could be when people went into the ice cream shop downstairs. Customers milled around outside in a way that they never hung around outside his Bristol flat. He found it all quite disturbing. Every noise made him leap out of his skin. He yearned for peace and quiet and knew the flat wasn't right for him as a permanent base. He needed to sell it, along with the shops and his mum and dad's house and find his own home… somewhere quiet where he could be alone with his books and his thoughts. Somewhere to sit and grieve and lament the love he'd lost and to work out what shape the future was without that love in it.

A FEW DAYS LATER, JOE WENT TO TALK TO THE MANAGERS OF the ice-cream shops. He told them that he was putting them up for sale, but wanted them to have the chance to buy them. He offered them huge discounts to help them out, earning himself more hugs, declarations of gratitude and tearful moments than he'd ever imagined knowing. It felt good. Helping people had made him feel alive and valuable. Even with the big discounts he'd given, he made a lot more money from all the sales. He would invest it wisely. He knew what it would be useful for one day, but not yet. Then he looked for somewhere to live, deciding on Mid Wales where he knew no one and could concentrate on writing to his heart's content.

He settled on a little village called Llandrindod Wells, miles from Bristol and a long way from his childhood home in Llanelli.

Once he had settled in, he set about writing as much as he could. He wanted to throw all his feelings, anger and emotion onto the page. He wanted to create plays that were wonderful works of art.

He worked night and day on his first play – a complicated work about reality and perception. It was an existentialist piece about understanding change and accepting that we know nothing about the future and what it holds. Ostensibly it was a play about a team of footballers who ran onto the pitch and arrived in a new dimension.

The place they arrived in was the real world, and the life before the tunnel was all their perceptions, all the baggage they brought to the world.

"The play is about how humans are so far inside the values they cling to that they never look outside them, meaning they operate in a world so coloured by their own views that it's not real," he wrote in a letter, pitching the idea to a theatre director. "The 11 men represent all 11 of men's failings and insecurities. The players are absolutely sure what the world is about until the day they run through the tunnel and onto the pitch. There they live a new enlightened life, a real life, and let go of all their nasty destructive prejudices."

Joe lay down his pen and smiled to himself as he thought about how this play had its roots in the school project he'd worked on with Michael, the young son of the B&B landlord. Michael's homework had been called 'A Bit of a Puzzler' and that's what he would call his play. He picked up his pen again. He would add a dramatic twist to the play and make the footballers turn on one another…they would have to choose one of their number – representing one of mankind's failings – to walk back through the tunnel into the flawed world they had escaped from. Yes.

He'd love to see his play being performed, but he desperately didn't want anyone to know he had written it. He had no desire for fame at all. He wanted no attention and had no real need for money. He simply wanted his work to fly. He needed a nom de plume and he knew straight away what name he wanted.

In his bag was the book he always carried with him: *Call of the Wild* – the novel his father gave him when he was little. His dad had kept the book from when he was a boy in Italy and had been fond of telling Joe how it had been through battles and been across countries and how he had read and reread the book to a young boy called Tom Gower. It had a faded yellow cover – the only possession his father had kept from when he was young. Joe flicked through it and saw the name that had coloured his childhood. Squadron Leader *Reginald Charters* – that was the name he would adopt. He would become Reginald Charters.

Chapter 24

2018

"That was quite funny," said Simon, as he pulled out all of the notes he'd made, reminding himself of exactly where he was before his kind decision to buy snacks had resulted in everyone in the group almost having synchronised heart attacks. No one else in the group laughed. "Well, it was funny from my point of view – coming in here to find you all crouched on the floor in pitch darkness. Jolly funny."

While he shuffled papers, I helped myself to another slice of the angel cake that Simon had bought: it was pink, pretty and very sweet so suited my inner seven-year-old down to the ground. I teamed it with a glass of wine and felt all set up for the afternoon.

No one else at the table seemed remotely interested in any of the snacks Simon had made such an effort to provide which, again, suited me down to the ground.

It was a mystery to me that anyone could sit there, all relaxed, while there were uneaten snacks lying on the table. I found it hard to concentrate on anything when there were cakes, crisps and biscuits within arm's length, regardless of how full I was.

The good news was that there seemed to be more of a buzz in the room now, after we'd had a break, or perhaps it was the bonding experience of fearing that the house was haunted by the ghost of Reginald Charters. People were more animated, there was murmuring and chatting, and less concern and frustration with the whole thing.

I turned to Matt who was sitting next to me and smiled.

"This is amazing, isn't it?" he said. "I mean – I wonder who on earth he was, and what this is about."

"Did you have any luck finding things out?" I asked him.

"No one in the family has heard of Reginald Charters," he said. "But I think I can understand why I've been given this clue. I've got a sort of inkling about my great Grandfather, but it might be nothing. I'll go through it all when we get started. How about you?"

I told him that I called Mum earlier and she was no use at all. She said we had no theatre types in the family and no connections to a taxi ride, a nurse or a B&B in Bristol.

I looked around the room, wondering whether anyone apart from Matt had found out anything that could take us further in our struggle to unlock the mystery. As I scanned the room I noticed that Julie had moved and was now sitting next to Mike. He had his arm round the back of her seat like a teenage boy on a cinema date in the 1950s, his fingers lightly touching her shoulders, subtly edging down the line of her bra strap.

Julie had reapplied all her makeup, and looked like she was

heading out to a top London nightclub not sitting in a rather dismal, ancient room in a farm masquerading as a B&B in the middle of nowhere. Still, who could blame her? Mike was gorgeous and Julie was incredibly beautiful when she was all done up. I was transfixed. Until she turned and saw me staring and I was forced to pull my head away so quickly that I almost gave myself whiplash.

I wondered what it must be like for Sally. Fancy growing up with a sister as beautiful as that. Her teenage years must have been torture. There were four years between them and such a distance in terms of how they looked…their body shapes, hair, the glossy skin, that star quality; Julie had it all. How horrible it must have been for Sally seeing her younger sister turn into such an incredible beauty. I was glad I didn't have siblings; I wouldn't have been able to control my jealousy if I'd had to grow up with someone like Julie.

"Right, let's go through everything, then," said Simon. "Mary – would you like to make notes?"

"Sure," I said, though I was far from sure. I'm not very good at practical things like this, and it was very likely I'd forget to write down something crucial and ruin everything.

"Here's some paper," said Matt, pushing a pad towards me. "Just shout if you want any help."

"Thank you," I said, noticing what lovely hands he had – very big and hairy. I like a man with proper man's hands.

"Shall we come to you first, Matt?" asked Simon.

"Oh, OK. Well, mine was a bit of a strange one because I just got a taxi receipt with a smile emoji on and something like a medical cross. I talked to Mum and Dad, and they said that my granddad was born in Bristol but then they moved to Wales when Grandad was a baby."

"Ah right. Was your dad someone who took taxis a lot? Or your grandad?"

"No," said Matt. "But my great grandad was a taxi driver."

"Oh," said everyone in the room.

"Ooooh," said Simon. "That is interesting. Did your grandfather work as a taxi driver in Bristol?"

"No, my great grandfather, not my grandfather."

"Oh," we all chorused in disappointment.

"Then he's probably too old for our calculations, isn't he?" I said.

"Yes, I guess so," said Matt. He looked quite dejected. Clearly he thought he would help the investigations with his revelation that his great grandfather was a taxi driver.

"Well, let's work it out," said Mike, taking his arm from around Julie's shoulders and leaning his elbows onto the desk. How old are you, Matt, if you don't mind me asking?"

"I'm 19."

"Write that down, Mary," instructed Mike in an aggressive tone.

"Certainly, Your Lordship," I replied. Mike glanced at me before turning his attention back to Matt.

"Do you know how old your dad is?"

"Yes, he is, like, 42 or 43. It was his 40th birthday a few years ago. Do you want me to find out exactly how old he is?"

"No, don't worry about that for now. So, how old would your grandfather be then? Do you have any idea?"

"Yes, I know it's his 70th birthday in a few weeks, because we're going to have a party."

"Great. OK then so that would make your great grandfather around 95-ish, would it?"

"I don't know, he died about 15 years ago, when I was little."

"Right," said Mike. "Sorry to hear that." He was leaning forward on his elbows. "I think this works though. Let's say your great grandad would be about 90, shall we?"

"Yes, I guess that would be about right."

"Then we need to work out what year he was born. Mary, can you work out what 2018 minus 90 comes to."

"Well, um," I said, rather taken aback by request for maths to be done. I didn't sign up for this. "I think it's 1928," I said, thanking the good lord for calculators on iPhones.

"Right, so what's the year on your taxi receipt?"

"It says 1976."

"So your great grandad would have been 48 in 1976?"

There were murmurs around the table.

"If that's what it works out at," said Matt. "I don't really know. I'm not very good at maths."

"I think that's right," said Mike. "Could you do us a big favour and ring your parents now and ask whether your great grandfather was likely to have been a taxi driver in Bristol in 1976?"

Matt picked up his phone and rang his parents, he spoke in Welsh to them but I could hear him say "1976" and various other words that translated into English. Eventually he put his hand over the receiver and addressed the group: "Yes, my great grandfather would have been working as a taxi driver in Bristol at that time."

"Bloody hell, I'm a genius," said Mike. "I should be in the sodding FBI."

"Write all that down," said Simon, glancing over at the pad as I did so.

"No, no… Not about Mike being a genius…don't write that – just everything to do with Matt."

I scribbled out the genius remark and wrote down the details about ages and years. Then I looked up at Simon.

"This is good," he said. "Matt – before you hang up – can you just check with your parents whether your great grandfather mentioned anything happening in 1976? There's the medical cross on the receipt, so possibly involving a hospital or doctors?"

Matt spoke in Welsh again and shook his head.

"They don't know," said Matt.

"OK," said Simon. "Could you ask them to call you if they think of anything that happened in 1976, anything at all? Also – can you tell me what your great grandfather's name was?"

Matt spoke briefly then put down his phone and said his great grandfather's name was Fred Radex. We all broke into a round of applause. I don't know why really. We'd discovered that Matt's great grandfather drove a taxi in Bristol in the 1970s, but we had no idea who Reginald Charters was, and didn't seem all that much closer to finding out, to be honest. I took a large sip of wine and helped myself to another slice of angel cake. It seemed rude not to.

"Julie and Sally – let's come to you next. Did you have any luck with your investigations?"

It was Sally who spoke, as we all knew it would be. The chances of Julie having bothered to make any calls were so remote as to be unworthy of consideration.

"Well, yes, I also had some luck," said Sally, and I saw Julie look up in amazement. "You'll remember that my sister and I had cuttings which related to nurses in 1976. Well, it turns out that my mum was a nurse then and…I never knew this…but she worked in Bristol."

"OK," said Simon. "Well, that's interesting. Very interesting. Did anything happen that she can remember from then?"

"She was only in Bristol at the beginning of her career, then she met my dad and they moved to Coventry then to Ascot before I was born, but she does remember a few things."

We all leaned forward a little in our seats.

"One thing she said she remembers is a big fight in the Students' Union when Bristol Uni played Gloucester Uni at rugby. It was a real grudge match and they were fighting in the bar afterwards. A load of rugby players came in to A&E with glass in their faces – she said that was horrible. That was one of the worst things she had to deal with because so many of them were badly hurt.

"Another thing she remembers is a black guy being attacked in a racist attack – it was awful. He died and Mum was devastated. She went to the funeral. His name was Ricky. The other thing was a guy who she found in the street who'd been attacked for being gay. They are the things she remembers but definitely none of those people was called Reginald. She says she thinks the gay guy was called Joe but she's not sure."

"What's your mum's name?" asked Simon.

"It's Daphne," said Sally. "Daphne Bramley."

There was a silence in the room and I scribbled down everything that had been said. What to make of all this? It didn't seem like it was forming any coherent picture.

"Perhaps the taxi driver was rushed to hospital? Or perhaps the taxi driver was one of the guys at the rugby bash at the university?" offered Simon.

"No, because the taxi driver was in his mid-40s," I said. "It would be unlikely."

"No one in my family's ever been to university," said Matt.

"How old is your mum, Julie?" asked Simon.

"She's 63."

"Right, so in 1976 she would have been?" He was looking at me but before I could reach for my phone, he'd worked it out. "Ah, 21," he said. "Write it down, Mary. And can you read back what we know so far?"

"Well, um – yes. We've got a taxi driver from Bristol and a nurse from Bristol who are related to people in the room and correspond with the clues that have been left, but Reginald's name has not come up at all in connection with either of them.

"Fred is no longer with us, so it's hard to get further information on his time as a taxi driver in the 1970s, but Daphne says she remembers three significant occurrences from her time in Bristol – a huge fight involving university rugby players in a bar, a racist attack and a homophobic attack.

"Daphne thinks the black guy was called Ricky, but she's not sure. She thinks the gay man was called Joe."

"Right," said Simon. "Have you got anything to add at all, Mary?"

I explained that I didn't. The advert for the playwriting course meant nothing to anyone in the family.

"I'm sorry," I kept saying. "It's really frustrating but Mum and Dad can't think of anything at all."

"Don't worry, Mary. Well, I'll run through mine, shall I? So, my father was a theatre director. He died about 20 years ago, but according to my mum, whose memory isn't the best, he worked with lots of up-and-coming writers and encouraged university students to write for the theatre. What I don't understand, though, is how this all comes together. My cutting is dated '1977' so if we are going to take a literal interpretation of all this – Reginald went on some sort of playwriting course in 1973, then in 1976 something happened involving a nurse and a taxi driver, then a year later he was somehow involved in this long list of theatre productions, most of which appear to be in some way linked to my father."

"Oh God, this is interminable," said Julie, from her position in the nook of Mike's arm. "How the hell are we supposed to come to any sort of conclusion?"

"Don't worry, angel," said Mike, gently stroking the top of her head. "Shall I go through mine?"

"Yes, yes, of course," said Simon, who'd clearly forgotten all about Mike. "I had a cutting of a B&B stuck over a map of Bristol. It's clear to me why I've got this – my mum and dad ran a B&B in Bristol for most of their lives. The date on it is 1976, and they were definitely running a B&B then. Unfortunately, my dad's died and mum, Sarah, is in a home with Alzheimer's, so I can't add any more than that."

Simon shook his head and looked out of the window across the fields. What was this all about? Why were they in Wales? Who were all these people gathered here today, and – most importantly of all – who in God's name was Reginald Charters?

Chapter 25

2018: REGINALD'S HOUSE IN WALES

REGINALD HAD HAD A PRETTY DECENT LIFE. HE COULDN'T complain. Perhaps not the sort of life that many people would choose for themselves; a life largely devoid of human contact and social activity. His had been a life devoted to writing.

"Have you brought anyone with you?" asked the doctor, sitting next to Reginald and trying not to catch his eye. The doctor had done this a hundred times…had this conversation with all manner of different patients, but it never got any easier. It was particularly difficult with this gentleman who seemed to hate hospitals and refused to be admitted for treatment.

"No, I'm on my own," said Reginald. "But don't worry – I'm fine. Just tell me what's going on, and let me get out of here. Tell me the truth."

"It's end stage. I'm sorry, Reginald, but it's spread and

there's nothing more we can do to stop the cancer. We can give you all sorts of drugs to keep you out of pain and we can make sure you sleep properly at night, but there's nothing we can do to prolong your life."

Reginald nodded impassively. "How long have I got?"

"Weeks," replied the doctor. "A month at most. I'm sorry. I wish I had different news. Cancer is a bastard…it's in your lymph nodes – it's spreading throughout your body."

Reginald smiled at the doctor and thanked him for his honesty.

"I'm sorry," repeated the doctor.

"It's not your fault," said Reginald.

They were at a politeness impasse, so Reginald stood up, shook the oncologist's hand and left.

"We can get you drugs for the pain," the doctor called after him. "You don't have to suffer, and we have counsellors to talk to, people who will help you."

"I'm not in pain," said Reginald, smiling. "But I'm very grateful for your concern, and I'm indebted to you for everything you've done to help me."

"A cancer specialist will call you, just to check you're OK and see whether there's anything we can do," said the doctor.

"You're very kind," repeated Reginald as he strode towards the door. He wished to waste no more time. Small-talk was all very well and good, but if he had just three or four weeks left, he needed to get cracking – he had so much to do and the last place he wanted to be was in a bloody hospital.

First, he needed to go to the private detective agency on Llandrindod Wells High Street. He strode in and announced that he needed to talk to someone urgently.

"Shall I make an appointment for you?" asked the receptionist. "We have lots of time next week."

"I'll wait," he said. "I can't come back next week; I don't know whether I'll be alive then."

"Oh," said the receptionist, looking alarmed. "I'll call Mr Dillon."

She shuffled off into some back room, then came out smiling.

"Mr Dillon is with a client but he will see you when he's finished. Can I get you a tea or coffee or anything?"

"I'm fine. Thank you for offering, though, that is most kind of you."

He sat in the waiting room and thought about every-thing...all the incredible plays he'd written but never taken credit for, all the friends he could have met and the lovers he could have enjoyed. But then – if he'd lived a normal life, he wouldn't have the body of work he'd created. And he could easily make everything right again in death – take ownership of the plays that he was so proud of, and take responsibility for saying 'thank you' to those people who'd made his life more bearable. And he'd share his plays with the people who meant so much to him....as a final act.

Mr Dillon emerged and announced that his name was Paul, though Reginald had no plans to address him in such a casual way. He was a rather smart-looking man, not what Reginald was expecting at all. He'd expected a chain-smoking, ill-fitting suit kind-of-guy...maybe with egg stains down his tie, certainly pot-bellied, and not wearing a neat, light blue lamb-swool jumper, smart trousers and shiny shoes. His hair was cut into a respectable short back and sides and he wore owlish glasses on his face. He looked clean cut, respectable. You'd never have guessed he was a private detective…which was useful really.

"You told my receptionist that you might be dead next week. Is someone threatening you?" he asked. "Do you fear for your life? I'm happy to help, if you are, but my suggestion is always that the first point of call should be the police. If you want me to contact the police and work with them, I can but I'd strongly advise police involvement. Unless the fears you have for your life are because of something you have done that is not entirely legal. Is that the situation?"

"No, no, no," said Reginald, smiling at the thought of him doing something illegal. "Thank you for your advice but even if I were about to be stabbed through the neck I wouldn't want the police involved. I'm not a fan of the boys in blue. No – the reason I told your receptionist that I had to see you urgently was because I'm dying."

"Oh, Mr Charters, I'm so sorry."

"No – don't feel sorry for me, I'm perfectly fine. I have been ill with cancer for a while and now have a few weeks to live. What I need from you is for you to find some people from my past. I've led a very quiet life, Mr Dillon, I've not made friends, I've locked myself away, but before I became a hermit, I was treated to great human kindness by some people, and I would like to leave their descendants all the money I have. I suspect some will be untraceable but I would like you to do your best."

"And you need this done quickly?" asked Mr Dillon.

"I want it done within the week and I will pay handsomely for the speed at which I am expecting you to work."

"OK," said Mr Dillon. "We'll certainly try. I can put a few operatives on the case and we'll see how we get on. I can report back to you in a couple of days. Are all the people in this country, or are we looking abroad?"

"At the time I knew them they lived in Wales and Bristol. They could live anywhere by now."

"We'll start the research and keep an open mind," said Mr Dillon. "We'll come back very soon with everything we have. Now, can I take some details from you?"

"There's something else," said Reginald. "It's the youngest descendants of these people that I am planning to leave my money to: the youngest descendants who are over 16. I'd like it to mirror one of the scenes from my play: *Youngest Child* – have you heard of it?"

"No, I haven't," said Mr Dillon. "I didn't realise you were a writer. I'm not much of a theatre-goer."

"That's a shame. Yes – I'm a writer. Not that anyone knows, of course – I've hidden my whole life. I've simply never spoken about my plays before. You're the first, Mr Dillon. I wanted to write without judgement and fear. Now, though, as I'm dying, I feel differently and want the world to know. That's why I'm telling you. My dying wish is to celebrate the kindness shown by individuals and to celebrate the plays I wrote but never claimed. All the money from the plays will go to charity. We'll come on to that though – I'm being very distracted, Mr Dillon, I do apologise – we have so much to get through. I didn't mean to bore you with talk of my plays."

"No problem at all. I'm happy to help you do whatever you want."

"Thank you. Now, where was I? Oh yes, I would like to have videos of the youngest children as well, and any information about how they live their lives today."

Mr Dillon wrote everything down. "We can try and video them in a public place," said Mr Dillon. "I'll talk to the operatives and explain your request and they will call you with any updates."

"One other thing," said Reginald. "I don't have a phone."

"No mobile? No problem, if you let us have your landline, we'll call you on that."

"No mobile, no landline," said Reginald. "I will need you to come to my flat every morning at 10am to update me. I will pay all costs, all fees, and I will tip you wildly if you can make my dying wish come true."

"We're very good at what we do, Mr Charters. If anyone can do it, we can. Do you want to let me have all the information you have?"

"Of course," said Reginald, feeling his mood lighten. He'd been rather dreading this encounter. Decades of self-enforced solitary confinement had left him ill-prepared to talk to people, motivate them to help him or even look them in the eye. He felt it had gone rather well though, and as Mr Dillon went to call the receptionist to take down the details of all the potential recipients, Reginald sat back in his seat and thought about how much he wished he could be there when they received the news that they'd each been left a small fortune.

Chapter 26

At 10am the next morning there was a loud knock on the door.

Excellent. Reginald liked people who were good timekeepers. He walked slowly to the door and swung it open. He hadn't been feeling very well that morning which was unusual for him. He'd coped well with the cancer symptoms but today he'd felt dreadful, achy, slow and – well – ill. Still, the sight of Mr Dillon and two other men on the doorstep lifted his spirits.

"Come in," he said. "Can I get you gentlemen a cup of tea?" As he posed the question, he realised he probably had no tea, certainly he had no milk…milk made him feel quite sick. He'd not bought it for months.

"No thank you," said Mr Dillon. "We're fine. Let me introduce Bob Kiffin and Mark Bow."

"Nice to meet you, gentlemen. Now, the important issue – do you have any news for me?"

"We do," said Mark or Bob, Reginald couldn't remember

who was who now. His memory was ridiculous. He had to write everything down or he forgot it immediately.

"So, you asked us to track down the youngest living descendants of six people: Andrew Marks, a former university lecturer at Bristol University who became a good friend, a taxi driver called Fred Radex, a nurse called Daphne Bramley, an owner of a bed and breakfast in Bristol called Nicholas Sween, a theatre producer called Alastair Blake, and any descendants of the Gower family who owned Gower Farm and then moved to North Wales. So far we have managed to find the descendants of two of those people."

"Oh, that's wonderful," said Reginald, clapping his hands together. The men could see how delighted the sick, frail old man looked and felt a buzz of excitement that they'd been able to bring him such joy.

"First, I've found the two daughters of Daphne Bramley... they are called Julie and Sally. Would you like to hear more about them? One is four years older than the other but I've got videos of both because we didn't know we were going to find the younger one when we videoed the older one."

"Yes please," said Reginald, sitting back in his seat.

They played a video on a laptop, it showed a very smart, beautiful woman striding down the street towards a glitzy office, she swung the door open then became distracted by someone she knew, and let it swing into the face of the person behind her. Next there was footage of the detectives talking to people outside the building. Those who knew Julie didn't appear to have very much to say about her that was good.

"Goodness, she doesn't look like much fun," said Reginald, crossing his arms across his chest as it dawned on him, for the first time, that he might be leaving a load of money to very unworthy recipients.

"No one had a good word to say about her. Everyone we talked to described her as 'arrogant', 'jumped up' and 'entitled'. The sister is different, though, would you like to see the next video?"

"Yes please."

A rather bigger, very plain lady was getting out of a car and heading towards a school, carrying bags as she spoke to children and chatted to teachers.

"We couldn't video the children without the school or their parents' permission, but they all love Sally. Other teachers didn't say much and it was hard to video them without them worrying about us videoing any children, but they were all very complimentary about Sally. She sounds like a down-to-earth, warm woman."

The clip had stopped with Sally's face frozen on it.

"My goodness, she resembles her mother," said Reginald. "Exactly like Daphne. That's how I remember her. She had such a soft voice and she looked like that. My goodness, it's like going back in time. She's the older one, is she?"

"Yes," said Mr Dillon. "I'm aware you want us to invite the youngest children, so we'll dismiss her."

"No, no – don't. Invite them both and I'll have some fun… create a bit of mischief like I did in *A Bit of a Puzzler*. I don't suppose you've heard of that, have you?"

"I'm afraid not. I really should go to the theatre more – you mentioned one of your plays before."

"Indeed," said Reginald. "My most successful plays will be coming to life after my funeral. And there will be big drama, BIG drama. How about that?"

"Yes, very good," said Mr Dillon. "Now, do you want us to talk to Daphne herself? It won't be hard. She and Sally live near one another in Ascot. We know Daphne gave up nursing years ago and moved out of Bristol when she met her husband to be. He's dead now and Daphne is retired."

"Oh that's lovely of you, but – no. The greatest way to repay a debt is to look after the youngest children."

"A line from your play?"

"Yes, Mr Dillon," said Reginald. "Very good."

Paul Dillon smiled, and thought he really should take his wife Daisy to the theatre soon, to see one of Reginald's plays.

"The other person we've found is Mike Sween, Nicholas Sween's son."

"Mike?" said Reginald, his face was alive with happiness and memories of the past. "Michael. My goodness, I did his homework with him and the story we wrote became the basis of my greatest play. Michael – such a sweet boy."

"We have a video," said Mr Dillon, fiddling with his laptop until an image of a handsome young man filled the screen. "We asked him what he thought of late-night pop music concerts being held at Twickenham – he lives there," said Mr Dillon. "Just to – you know – get him talking. This was his reply…"

"Thanks for asking," said the handsome face, bursting with confidence and a hint of narcissism. "I think music concerts are great, exactly what we need to liven up the area. I'm all in favour."

The clip came to an end.

"We don't have anything on what he's like – there were no neighbours around and he works for SKY so we couldn't get near to his work because of security gates – but we'll keep trying. He was very nice and helpful to our pretend camera-man, if that helps?"

"No – that's fine. I just wanted to see them. Any idea what happened to Nicholas? He was a nice guy."

"I'm afraid he died. His wife Sarah is still alive though."

The three men left, leaving Reginald to contemplate what to do… It simply hadn't occurred to him that the descendants of the fine people who had helped him years ago wouldn't be decent or worthy of his charity. Julie seemed most unpleasant. He had a clever idea about how to deal with her…an idea that would give a grand twist to the whole thing. But what if the others turned out to be equally unpleasant creatures? Should some get more money than others based on how they lived their lives? But that didn't suit him at all. He didn't want to be judge of their lives. Who was he to do that? It was very complicated.

The next day Mark and Bob returned, this time without Mr Dillon, and the day after that, with him again.

They were managing to locate the descendants of everyone who had helped him. Fred Radex, the taxi driver, had a great grandson who still lived with his mum and dad – he was sweet and kind and over 16. His life was about to be transformed.

Simon Blake, son of Alastair, the man who allowed him to write and earn without ever revealing his identity, had been found. Reginald knew that Alastair had died because he'd worked with him until his death six years ago, and he could easily have found his descendants without too much trouble, but he liked the fact that Mr Dillon's men were doing the whole thing for him and providing him with videos of his son Simon. He doubted whether anyone would ever understand just how much Alastair had helped him by allowing him to write plays and see them produced and staged without ever having to be named as the writer. Alastair went to all the meetings on his behalf and allowed Reginald to write all day and never be forced to see anyone or talk to anyone except Alastair. When Alastair died, Reginald stopped writing…that was how symbiotic their relationship had become.

ON THE FOURTH DAY ONLY ONE OF THE INVESTIGATORS CAME to see him – Bob Kiffin, a young buck who had the bearing of an over-eager estate agent itching for a sale in order to impress his girlfriend. He had a video with him of a lady called Mary Brown – a jolly, fat woman who turned out to be the youngest living descendant of Andrew…beautiful, lovely Andrew. He watched the video of the lady in her DIY store, messing around with the plants – peering through them to entertain children, laughing all the time, and eating when she wasn't, and he thought how different she was from Andrew – the man he'd loved so much. Andrew taught him what love was, but he could never be described as jolly or happy.

"How are they related?" asked Reginald.

"Quite distantly, I'm afraid. He doesn't have his own children but his brother adopted a boy and the boy's daughter is Mary."

"Oh," said Reginald. He felt disappointed that she wasn't a blood relative, but he knew Andrew only had one brother and if that brother adopted rather than had his own children, then the bloodline ended there, there was nothing he could do.

He looked back at the screen where Mary was hiding behind a small potted privet hedge to eat a chocolate bar. "Yes, that's fine," he said. It wasn't so much who he gave the money to as a gesture of thanks for the past that he and Andrew had shared.

"Any news at all on Andrew?" he asked.

"He died 10 years ago," said the man. "I think he was gay,

actually, not that that's relevant, just didn't know whether you knew."

Not relevant? His whole life had been strangled by the relevance of being gay in rural 1970s England.

"I'm gay too," said Reginald, determined to say it proudly and openly for the first time in his life. "Andrew stood by my side when I first came out. He allowed me to be gay, he told me it was OK to be myself. He supported and nurtured me. He changed me from a shy and confused boy to a happy man."

"Cool," said the detective. "Andrew sounds amazing."

No judgement, no disgust. Perhaps the world had moved on since 1976.

"There's only one problem now," he said. "We can't find the Gower family anywhere. Well – we can – but not the right family. We've found Gowers in North Wales but we've not found any who moved there from South Wales, and used to own Gower Farm. Paul's there at the moment, and Mark Bow is talking to people living near Gower Farm. I suspect the man and woman died and had no children."

"I'm sure they had children - a boy called Tom. Tom Junior he used to be called. Please keep looking."

Once the investigator left, Reginald lay on the sofa and drifted off to sleep, he dreamt of happy times: Andrew's warmth; sunshine flickering through the leaves on long walks to the park; his mother's gorgeous smile…

Chapter 27

"Mr Charters, are you OK?"

Bang. Bang. Bang.

"Mr Charters?"

Reginald stirred in his position on the sofa. He took a minute to work out where he was and what the terrible noise was before he struggled to his feet and tried to move slowly towards the door, but he couldn't do it, his legs collapsed beneath him.

BANG! Much louder now, then suddenly people were in the room.

"Mr Charters, can you hear me? It's Paul Dillon here. We've called an ambulance; it will be here soon."

"Not an ambulance," he said. "I can't go to hospital."

But his voice was a whisper that no one heard. And he fell straight back to sleep.

"Good morning, Mr Charters." A stout nurse with

appalling skin was breathing down on him and making him feel quite nauseous. She lifted his arm to take his pulse, counting under her breath. "OK. Doctor will be here soon," she said.

"Where's Mr Dillon?" he asked.

"I don't know a Mr Dillon," she said.

"He brought me in. I need to talk to him. Please, it's very important, he's helping me to fulfil my dying wish."

She looked back at the sad old man who'd already soiled the bed twice.

"I'll find out," she said.

"He works as a private detective."

After what seemed like an interminable wait, Mr Dillon appeared at his bedside with his reliable associates. He smiled when he saw them – Paul, Bob and Mark – his Three Muske-teers; they were the closest he'd come to having friends for decades. He noticed that Mr Dillon was carrying a bunch of grapes. Perhaps he should have made more of an effort over the years. Friends had always seemed like such hard work. When you paid for people's time, like he was doing with these three, it made it all much less complicated.

"Have you found Tom?" he asked. "Or Tom's children? Anyone connected to the Gowers?"

"No," said Paul Dillon. "I've been out there for days, as has Mark. We've found nothing, it's like the whole family has disappeared into the ether."

"Really? But how could that happen? I don't understand."

"It can take a while to find people, I can carry on searching but it might take longer than…well, you know – it might take a while."

"Keep searching, never stop searching," said Reginald. "Now I need you to do something else for me – I need you to get a solicitor here ASAP so I can sign over power of attorney to you."

"But you don't know me. You can't do that."

"I know you better than any other person alive today. I trust you."

While Mr Dillon reluctantly went in search of a lawyer, Reginald subjected himself to test after test from box-ticking doctors with clipboards and charts. He was injected and fussed over. They would take him out of pain, they would keep him clean and they would all know that any day now he would die. Probably sooner rather than later, Reginald suspected. He could no longer walk, nor could he feed himself, and the pain of swallowing and shortness of breath combined to make him feel vulnerable and scared. Not scared of death, but scared of not having everything in place for death.

When Mr Dillon arrived back with a lawyer, the form signing began, and Reginald signed over money and instructions to the amiable private detective in the presence of the serious-looking solicitor.

"Now, I need you to find me someone who can produce a video for me. The video will incorporate all the short films you've made of the people who will be in my will."

Dillon sent his assistant, Mark, to investigate. While he was gone, Reginald sat back against the pillows.

"I would like to invite the people you've found to the funeral," he said. "I want them to be the only people there – they represent the only people in my life who really cared."

"Sure," said Dillon. He wanted to add that he had grown to care a little, and that he wouldn't have broken down the door to his flat and got him to hospital if he didn't care. He wanted to add that the doctors and nurses all cared. There were lots of people who cared about him, if only he would abandon his deeply held views that he was alone in the world, and look around him he'd see that. But the man was sick and frail. He'd just help him all he could and do his best to fulfil the man's dying wish.

REGINALD STEELED HIMSELF. ALL HE HAD TO DO NOW WAS make this simple video then he could slip away. He hoped that the money he was leaving to people would enable them to see the world…and live much fuller lives than he had.

"I'm going to create a bit of mischief in my will. You hear that, Mr Dillon. Not everyone who comes to the funeral will get money, you see."

"Right," said Dillon.

"All the information is in that envelope I gave you. You know what to do? You pass all this on to the people who come to the funeral, OK. Remember the envelopes we talked about. Use that solicitors on the High Street in Llanelli, next to Joe's Ice Cream Parlour – Beddows and Plunkett and use Degs Funeral Service in Llanelli. It's all in the letters I gave you."

"Yes – I've got all your notes here about which people to use, Reg. Don't worry."

"OK, then we just need to make this video to show after the funeral, and everything is sorted. Agreed?"

"Yes, just the video. Are you up to recording it now?"

"Yes, I'm ready. I've been practising for this moment all my life. Let's go then."

Mr Dillon straightened the sheets on the bed so that Reginald looked as respectable as possible.

"When you're ready," said the young nurse who had been given the duty of holding the iPhone to capture his words.

"Can they see me and hear me?" he asked.

"Yes, all ready to go," she said.

"Hold it up, nurse, and make sure they can hear what I'm saying."

"Don't you worry," she said. "We can hear you loud and clear."

Chapter 28

2018: GOWER FARM HOTEL

I WOKE UP AND KNEW IMMEDIATELY THAT I WASN'T TUCKED UP in my lovely, comfortable, modern bed at home. I glanced at the terrible decor and the tiny window next to the bed through which a cold breeze was seeping. I pulled back the thick, floral curtains to check that I hadn't left it open but – no – it was just old, and allowing a horrible freezing draught to come in. I fiddled with the handle to try and pull it tighter.

Then I remembered.

Oh God.

It was like I'd been shot in the stomach.

Shit.

I had to make a speech…about someone I'd never met, but who held me in such high esteem that he was insistent I come to his funeral. How the hell do you write a speech for such an occasion? Bugger. I wished I'd written it last night, but after the lengthy late-night discussions I'd been too tired by the time I got to bed. At least we had a theory now about why we were at the funeral…however vague it was. We'd decided that Reginald was an ageing actor who'd lived in Bristol and dated a nurse who he met in a taxi. It didn't feel substantial enough to be worthy of a £1 million reward but it was the best we could do.

Now I had to write a bloody eulogy. I pulled out my laptop and googled 'funeral speeches'.

There was a brilliant site which listed touching eulogies that were perfect for funerals. They gave loads of examples of great speeches for mums, dads, husbands, babies and friends, but – perhaps unsurprisingly – there were no examples of eulogies you could make about someone you'd never met before and knew absolutely nothing about.

I clicked on the example of a eulogy to a friend and cut and pasted it into a Word document. I would go through the eulogy and change it so it related to Reginald. Quite how I would do this I had no idea; I would have to keep it vague. I scurried through the document, cutting and changing and throwing out detailed sentences and throwing in attributes that felt appropriate until I had a short speech that I thought I could deliver without causing offence. Since it didn't appear that anyone who had ever met him would be at the funeral, it didn't matter too much – there would be no one around to contradict me if I just made it all up. But I felt a strange loyalty to this man who had brought me to the strange hotel in the middle of nowhere, and introduced me to this odd collection of people. I wanted to do well by him even though I might never know why he had invited me.

I dressed in black and walked down to breakfast to meet the others. When I got to the dining room they were already there, sitting in silence, also dressed in black, eating cooked breakfasts. I took a seat next to Mike and Julie and ordered a full English.

"So, have you got your speech all written?" said Mike. "I don't envy you that at all."

"Kind of," I said. "I've got something written, but I've no idea whether it's any good."

"I'm sure it will be perfect," said Mike, as my huge breakfast arrived in front of me. There was fried bread, fried eggs, fried bacon, fried sausage, fried tomato, fried mushroom and black pudding. There were also beans and toast piled onto the plate and when I moved the toast I found fried potatoes nestling underneath it. This might be the greatest breakfast I'd ever had.

"Will you excuse us," said Mike, standing up, and pulling out Julie's chair. I noticed that Julie had no plate in front of her, and had been drinking a cup of boiled water. Where was the fun in that?

I finished my breakfast and waited in the lobby to be taken over to the church for the funeral service. I'd been told that I would be able to practice first, but no one came at 9am, so I waited with the others until 9.30am and walked over with them. There was a lot of smiling, encouraging and hugging me and telling me not to worry and how brave I was. With every kind word and compliment I felt more and more nervous about what I had to do. I clutched my notebook tighter as we followed the funeral director out of the hotel and towards the small church and graveyard opposite.

We walked in and all sat on the front pew. There were a few people scattered on the other pews.

"Who are they?" asked Mike. "I thought we were the only ones coming."

"No, no one here knows Reginald. They're locals who just come along to most funerals we hold here…for something to do. Except for those three men at the end of the pew over there. I don't think they are locals. They said their names are Paul Dillon, Mark Bow and Bob Kiffin."

I watched as the vicar walked to the front of the church, coughed gently, looked up and smiled.

I was kind of hoping that the vicar would say something personal about Reginald that I could echo in my speech, but - no such luck – instead of a warm, personal speech, the vicar thanked us all for coming and said he was pleased that everyone who Reginald had asked to be at his funeral was here, and he was delighted to hand over to me for the eulogy.

Shit.

I walked to the front and could feel five pairs of eyes boring into the back of my head. I looked down at my note-book and out to the congregation, seeing five people at the front, staring at me expectantly and around half a dozen other people dotted around the church. One was knitting, others sat stiffly in their best coats, waiting for me to start. The three men on the far pew had a look of genuine grief on their faces, but as far as I was aware, none of the people in this church knew, or had even met, Reginald.

I cleared my throat and began to read from my notebook.

"Thank you very much, everyone, for coming here today to remember Reginald Charters. I know he would be delighted that you are all gathered in this lovely church to honour him and say 'goodbye'." I paused. This was ridiculous. Reading out inanities was pointless. I needed to tell the truth.

"This is a very difficult talk to give," I continued. "Because I don't know Reginald. As far as I'm aware I've never met him, but I know that I am connected to him in some way. He asked for me and for the other five gathered in the front row to come to his funeral. I'll be honest – we don't know why he asked us. Last night we spent lots of time trying to work it out, but we still don't understand, not really.

"So this is a crazy situation and this is a very difficult speech to give. What I'd like to say to you, though, is that this whole experience has taught me a lot: it's taught me that the little things we do for one another really matter. Somewhere along the line, a relative of mine did something for Reginald that was so special that he sought to offer his gratitude by tracking me down and inviting me to the funeral.

"My relative might not even have understood how great a favour he did for Reginald. We might never find out what happened and why we are here. But we know that relatives of ours meant a huge amount to Reginald.

"It's the little things you do – the favours and kindnesses you perform that are the most important things, and can mean everything to someone.

"What our relatives did for Reginald clearly meant every-thing to him and I'm glad to be here today to remember him, and to be reminded that being good to people, being kind and thoughtful, is the most important thing. Thank you very much."

I walked back down to my seat, almost light-hearted with relief that it was all over. I'd winged it, but I'd been honest, and I had reflected the truth of Reginald in the spirit of every-thing we knew about him.

"Let us pray," said the vicar. I dropped my head and thought about Reginald Charters…whoever he was.

Chapter 29

"Come in and take a seat," said the solicitor, ushering us all into his meeting room where a large screen television stood in the corner. "I hope the funeral was OK. Please sit down and we'll get started."

We all shuffled along, undoing our black garments in the heat of the office and plonking ourselves onto wooden chairs set out in a line like at junior school.

There was tension, rather than excitement, in the air; we were finally going to find out exactly what this was all about. I think we were all a little about what we might hear. Why hadn't he just told us at the beginning what this was all about? Why did he try to make us guess? Perhaps there was a nasty sting in the tail and we were all about to be shot.

"OK. Well, it's my duty to inform you that we act for the late Mr Reginald Charters," said Huw. "We were contacted by his representative last week after his death from cancer. We were given specific instructions to contact you, as we did, and to gather you today for the funeral and for this reading of the will afterwards."

He was reading from a note, clearly left behind by Reginald.

"Mr Charters requested that I hand out envelopes to you, as I have. In the envelopes were clues as to why he had invited you. I am now asked to play this short film to you which will explain everything."

"How exciting," I muttered to Sally. She squeezed my leg affectionately and went to say something back to me, but before she could get the words out, an image burst onto the screen.

"Can they see me and hear me?" he was asking.

He was a very old, frail-looking man in a hospital bed.

"Hold it up, nurse, and make sure they can hear what I'm saying."

A grainy image of the late Reginald appeared in front of us.

"HELLO, I AM SORRY TO BE SO INTRIGUING, AND TO DROP hints and make you work hard to find out the truth," he said. "But I wanted you to be intrigued enough to listen carefully when I told you my story, my truth, and explain what these clues mean. And why I have chosen you to come to my funeral. If you'd just received a note in the post advising you of my passing and leaving you money, you'd not have taken in the magnitude of my story. So, I'm sorry for the subterfuge, but I think it was necessary in order to get your attention right from the very start.

"So, what should I say then? Well, first of all – you haven't worked it out, have you? No way will you have. No way at all. I couldn't resist giving you 20 hours to work it out, just like in my play *20 Hours to Save the World*. Have any of you seen it? Of course you haven't. If you have, you'd know that the world doesn't really blow up after 20 hours."

We all leaned forward in our seats, as if being physically closer to the television would make what we were being told somehow clearer. We were all fascinated.

"And just like in the play, you will inherit money regardless of whether you've been able to work out my link to you all. So that's good, isn't it? As I say, I only made you guess in order to capture your imagination. And for the sheer fun of it, of course.

"Right, I should stop waffling. My name is Reginald Charters, but I was born Joe Stilliano, my father, Marco Stilliano, came over to Wales during the war as an Italian prisoner and worked on Gower Farm."

There was a gasp from Huw. I turned to face him to see him staring at the screen, mesmerised. "Joe Stilliano? Marco's boy? Goodness!"

"I changed my name to Reginald Charters after I was badly beaten up for being gay. The year was 1976 and homosexuality had only been legalised nine years previously and was frowned upon. I was regularly spat at and glared at, and one day I was beaten so badly I thought I'd die. I couldn't possibly go to hospital or tell the police – I'd heard lots of stories about how homophobic those organisations were and how many young gay men reported crimes only to find themselves beaten up again by angry policemen. Oh, I know you're probably thinking that things like that never happen, but this was the 1970s – a very different time."

Reginald's voice was shaky but clear. He stopped and a

nurse gave him a sip of water out of what looked like a feeding bottle for a guinea pig.

"Sorry," he said. "I'm a sick, old man, as I'm sure you can see. Well, after I was beaten up, three people came to my aid: a taxi driver called Fred Radex found me and looked after me before he called Daphne Bramley. The two of them took me back to the B&B run by Nicholas and Sarah Sween and there they looked after me. I never repaid their kindnesses, but they saved my life, I've no doubt of that. I always promised to pay them back. And, as you'll know if you've read my play, *Youngest Child*, you go to hell if you don't help out the youngest child of anyone who does you a favour."

"Oh yes," said Simon, nodding frantically. "That's right – I remember the play now."

"Sally, Julie, Matt and Mike – I am going to pay you back now for what your relatives did for me," Reginald continued.

"There are two other people there – Mary and Simon. Let me tell you why you are here."

I could feel my heart beating inside my chest.

"Now, I've only loved one man, a gentleman called Andrew Marks. He made me feel wonderful…alive and worth something. He taught me who I was and what life was about and I loved him intensely for three years before he fell out of love with me. After I was beaten up, I ran away. I never said goodbye.

"Mary Brown – you are the closest family member to him. Andrew never had his own children but his brother, Carl, adopted a boy and that boy is your dad, Mary Brown."

"Oh blimey," I said. "Well I'd never have worked that connection out in a million years."

"I wished I'd said goodbye to Andrew and thanked him properly for loving me, but I didn't. The reason I didn't was because I was beaten up so badly that I withdrew from the world. I had nightmares every day after I was attacked and was left so terrified that weeks went past when I refused to leave the house. I should have asked for help but I didn't. What kept me going after I'd been loved by Andrew and physically saved by my three angels, was writing. I wrote and wrote, but I had no desire to attach my name to any of the pieces I wrote, so I changed my name to Reginald Charters after a character in a book that my father left for me, a book I loved very much when I was growing up. But then I realised I didn't want my new name to be famous either, so I met Alastair Blake, a theatre producer, and explained everything to him. He allowed me to write plays for him under a variety of names without telling anyone who the real creator was.

"I worked with Alastair for 30 years and managed to avoid all limelight and all contact with the theatre world. I wrote, I earned money – lots of money – but was never famous. Simon, I met you so many times when you were a boy, but you were never introduced to me. Your father kept my identity secret from everyone, even his family.

"He was a wonderful, wonderful man. He gave me the opportunity to do exactly what I wanted to do, and he put on plays I'd written that were scandalous at the time, he took the flak and gave me the money. Even when my plays were made into films – like when *A Bit of a Puzzler* was made into a film called *The Devil's Work* – my identity was kept secret." The writer of that play was Lorenzo Alberto – named after dad's best friend in the war. They were taken as prisoners of war together but lost touch when Lorenzo went back to Italy.

Reginald snorted with laughter at this stage, and started coughing wildly. A nurse offered him another drink out of the funny feeding bottle and he carried on.

"So, here you all are…my chosen ones. I've seen videos of you all – I know a little about you all. I believe that you are the youngest generation of the families I wish to support.

"My only disappointment today is that I couldn't track down anyone related to Tom and Irene Gower – the family who took my father in and supported and helped him. I will leave money for their family for when any of them is found. Someone has to be found. I want everyone to keep on looking…they saved my father's life. They were good people. Are you all good people? I hope so.

"So, the good news…my share in the branches of Joe's Ice Cream Parlour, which I sold decades ago, along with my income from being a playwright, has netted me well over £3 million. £1 million of that will be left in trust in the hope that relatives of Tom and Irene Gower can be found. They deserve that. It's what my father would want me to do. A million will be used to provide gifts for all those who have helped me to fulfil my dying wish. By the time all costs, debts and the funeral are taken care of, I estimate that I will have £1 million left that I would like to leave to you. I propose that I give each of you £200,000. How does that sound?"

There was a pause in the video while Reginald cocked his head to one side. We all did calculations on our fingers. Matt was the first to vocalise what we had all realised. "There are six of us, so that's not £200k each."

"Have you worked it out yet?" said Reginald as we were all mumbling and trying to do the basic mathematics.

"I couldn't part without one final bit of puzzling mischief, could I?"

A silence fell over the room as we all looked from one to the other.

"One of you won't be getting anything," he said slowly,

leaning in to the camera. "Just like in *A Bit of a Puzzler* you will all receive a huge amount of money except one of you, and you as a group will decide which person will go home empty-handed. That's why I asked you to stay for the day today. You have a choice to make.

"It's now around 11.10am, if my instructions have been followed properly. You have until 2pm to report back here without one person in the group. The person missing will be the one you all vote off. The person selected need not return. Then I might have another surprise for you. You can't vote for yourself, and you can't opt to share the money six ways – one of you has to be voted out."

Chapter 30

"Do we have to do this?" I asked the solicitor. "It's a really horrible thing to do."

"You heard what he said. It's one of the absolute conditions of the money being passed over."

"This is monstrous," said Julie, and for the first time in two days, I agreed with her. It also felt like it was needless and cruel.

"Please follow me," said the receptionist, opening the door to another room, and trying to lead us in.

"Where are we going?" asked Simon. "Can't we stay in here and make our decision?"

"Of course, you're more than welcome to stay here, but we have a boardroom with a large table in it, it's much better for discussing, deciding what you want to do."

"OK."

We were shown into a boardroom that had definitely seen better days – I didn't know what high-level negotiations took place there, but it was far from impressive. The only good news was that there was a large table full of snacks – I mean, proper snacks – the best snacks – potato skins dripping in melted cheese and bacon, chicken nuggets, sandwiches, crisps, dips, mini burgers and cones of fries. The BEST snacks. I wandered straight over and piled potato skins, crisps and chips onto my plate before realising that someone was talking to me. I glanced up to see them all seated, looking over.

"Are you joining us?" said Julie. "You had an enormous breakfast, surely you don't need any more food." She gave me a withering look as she spoke and raised her eyebrows at Mike as if to say 'look at the state of her'. I put the plate down on the side and went to join the group.

"Where's your food?" asked Simon.

"It doesn't matter," I said, even though it really, really did.

"No, seriously, Mary – where's the plate you had. What have you done with it?"

"Oh, don't worry – it's over there," I said, indicating the corner of the buffet where I'd dropped it suddenly under questioning from Julie.

Simon stood up and strode to the buffet, picked up my plate and brought it to me. He put it in front of me.

"There you go," he said. "Enjoy it, Mary. That looks delicious. Ignore Julie."

"How about we go back and say we all share the money that's there," said Julie. "Just force them to let us all have some."

"We can't – he'd probably make us all leave without anything," said Simon.

"Well, what on earth are we going to do then?" asked Julie. "This is so childish, there is no way we can eliminate one person. That's ridiculous."

"We will all have to vote. It's the only way to do it. Write the name of the person you think should not receive any money, and I will add them up and the person with the most votes is the one who has to leave," said Simon.

"We can't do that," said Julie.

"What else will we do?" I chipped in.

Julie glared at me. "Haven't you got potatoes to eat?" she said.

She really was the most unpleasant person. I was now damned sure I knew who I was voting for. Beautiful or not, she had to go.

"Hands up everyone who thinks the best thing to do is to write on a piece of paper the name of the person we wish to eliminate."

Every hand went up except Julie's. She nudged Mike aggressively until he took his hand down. Even with his forced change of mind, the result was clear.

"Then we vote. Does anyone want to say anything before we vote?"

"Hi, I hope you don't mind, but I would just like to say something," said Matt. "This has been the weirdest weekend of my whole life, and I was really worried about coming, and then when I saw how grown-up and posh everyone was, in this really elegant hotel, I got even more worried. But you've all been very kind."

He was bright red as he spoke. "And it's really good, isn't it, that our relatives helped this man when he was in great need. I've been thinking – would I do that? I really hope so. It makes me feel so proud, and even if I get voted off – I'm glad I came here. I'm really glad I met you."

"Here, here," said Simon, raising his glass. "To our relatives. May we be as kindly remembered as they have been."

"To our relatives," we all said, raising our glasses.

"And to Reginald," I added quickly.

"To Reginald," we all toasted again, then Simon took control, handing round pieces of paper. "I know we all think this is very unfair, but it was Reginald's wish, and this is Reginald's money."

Once everyone had received their piece of paper, Simon spoke:

"There is no need to identify yourself," he said. "All you need to do is write the name of the person that you think we should eliminate, and shouldn't receive any money."

I took my piece of paper and wrote "Julie Bramley" on it, and folded it up and put it into the envelope that was passed around the table. Not only was Julie the person I liked the least, but there were two sisters… If Sally wanted to, she could give Julie some money. If anyone else around this table was eliminated, they would receive no money at all.

Well, that's what I tried to convince myself of anyway, but – basically – I didn't like her. She was snappy and self-opinionated and just because she was born beautiful she thought she was better than everyone else. The envelope had arrived back with Simon.

"Now, I'm not sure how to do this – whether I should go through the envelope and work out who is the person who has to leave, or whether I should read out the names one by one."

"Read out the names," said Julie. "Then we know it's genuine."

I thought to myself that it was odd she suspected Simon would not be genuine. I could not think of a more reliable, honest man to conduct this bizarre procedure.

"Fair enough," said Simon. "If that's the way people feel, then I will make sure that it's all very transparent."

He put his hand into the envelope and pulled out a piece

of paper, unfolding it carefully. I knew that it would be a vote for Julie, as they all would be.

"The first vote is for you, Mary Brown," he said.

"Oh. Me?" I said. "Right, sure."

"Yes, sorry, Mary. The first vote is for you."

I could feel my heart beating in my chest and a dull ache developing in my stomach. It was nothing to do with fears about not getting the money. I've never been very money orientated. It was more about the fact that someone had thought I was the worst person in the group. How could they think that? What had I done wrong? Christ, I gave the speech at the funeral. I tried to be nice to everyone. I could feel tears pricking in the back of my eyes.

"Don't take it personally, Mary," said Simon. "It's just the ridiculous position we're in." The next name to be pulled out was "Julie", then another one: "Julie".

I was glad that the majority of people appeared to be voting for Julie, but all I could think about was the fact that someone had voted for me.

The Julies kept on coming.

Then "Simon".

Simon took the news that he'd been picked out as someone who shouldn't receive the money with a simple shrug.

All the rest of the names to be pulled out of the envelope said "Julie". We had decided.

"Are you really suggesting that I leave?" she asked, aggressive and confrontational.

"Yes," said Simon. "This is nothing to do with us, it's everything to do with Reginald. This is what he wanted; we are just obeying his wishes."

"It does seem very unfair," said Sally, leaping to her sister's defence. "Are you sure we shouldn't challenge it? Make a point of refusing to throw anyone out. Perhaps he's waiting to see whether we'll throw someone off and if we do, none of us will get any money. He might be playing games to see whether we stick up for the group as a whole? Julie's done nothing wrong, it seems so cruel."

"Yes," said Julie. "And anyway – you got a vote against you, Mary. Maybe you should leave? Or you, Simon."

"No," said Simon. "This is all getting very silly. You have the most votes and I'm afraid you are the person who has to leave."

"Fine, I'm going. I'd have gone anyway because this is an absolute farce. A waste of the weekend for nothing. The only good news is that I got to vote for Mary.

"I mean, look at the plate of food you had right now – should you really be eating all that food considering the weight you are? You're not even a blood relation of anyone who helped Reginald."

At this point Mike stepped up. "Come on, Julie, you're bang out of order here – just go." Julie left the room and we all sat there, shell-shocked.

"I think this is cruel," said Sally, as her sister left. "Very cruel."

It occurred to me, once she'd gone, that if Julie voted for me and therefore there was only one other vote that wasn't for her, it meant that either Mike or her sister had voted for her to go. It couldn't possibly be her sister so it must've been Mike. As we all prepared to walk back into the room without Julie, I turned to him and gave him the biggest smile I could muster.

Chapter 31

"Please, take your seats," said Huw, as we trooped back into the room. We all sat down exactly where we'd been sitting before, with Julie's seat empty.

"Thank you for making a decision. I know it must have been hard," he said. "Can I just confirm – Julie Bramley has not come back into the room with you, is that correct?"

"Yes," we mumbled, then Simon took the lead:

"Yes, I can confirm that Julie Bramley has not come back with us."

"OK, thank you very much. I'm going to show you the rest of the video now, then I need to take bank details from you and you're free to go."

He picked up the remote control, scowled at it then pressed the buttons on it like he'd never operated any technological equipment in his life before. Eventually, the screen burst into life and Reginald was back in the room.

"Hello," he said. "You're back! Without Julie I hope. Please tell me you're without Julie. Terrible error if you've thrown someone else to the dogs. So, that's all I've got for you. The clues were simply to make you think about my story and your relatives' places in it. To think about kindnesses you might perform. I wish you nothing but joy and happiness. Look after yourselves. Stay in touch with one another and have wonderful, fulfilling lives."

Then the picture went and Reginald was gone.

Huw walked to the front of the room. "Reginald died two hours after the video was made. He slipped away peacefully."

We sat in reverential silence for a moment, none of us quite sure how to react. We knew he'd died of course, we'd spent the morning at his funeral, but it was still moving to hear his final words and to know the details of his passing.

As we sat there, the solicitors' receptionist appeared at the back of the room and motioned to Mr Beddows to join her. He excused himself and walked over to her, and the sound of whispered Welsh filtered through the room. Then he walked back to the front.

"Ladies and gentlemen, you might have been aware of three men at the funeral, at the far side of the church. They are the private detectives who Mr Charters employed to track you down and fulfil his final wishes. They say they are happy to come in and talk to you about Reginald and tell you anything you might not know. Would that be of interest?"

"Oh yes," I said, as a chorus of 'yeses' followed mine. We'd not met anyone who knew Reginald, it would be great to find out what he was really like.

Huw excused himself and left the room, returning minutes later with three men in thick overcoats.

"These are the private detectives I mentioned. They dealt directly with Reginald and may be able to answer any questions you have."

"Sure, my name's Paul. It's lovely to meet you all. We work for a small private detective firm and were called by Reginald a couple of weeks ago and asked to find you. He didn't have much information about where you'd be or what chance we had, and – as you've heard – we couldn't track down any of the people related to Tom Gower, so we're still working on that. We spent a bit of time with Reginald and got to know him fairly well. We're happy to answer any questions you may have."

"Thank you," said Simon. "Would you mind explaining what happened? And – when he called you, what sort of guy was he?"

"Yes, of course. Well, the first thing to say is that he didn't call, because he didn't have a phone: no landline and no mobile. He came into the office and we had to go to his flat to update him.

"He was very old-fashioned, courteous and a little shy really. He was very nice – I warmed to him, but I felt he'd locked himself away for a long time and, as he was dying, he wished he hadn't. He used fake writers' names on his plays because he didn't want to deal with the attention that his plays would bring him and he regretted that and wanted it put right after his death. He's leaving all the royalties from them to charity.

"He also regretted that he lost touch with people who'd been very kind to him. That's why he wanted you to be here today and to inherit some of his money."

"Can I just ask you how we were chosen? Julie and Sally were here, but my older sister wasn't invited," said Mike.

"He asked me to track down the youngster descendants who were over 16."

"Ah, so it was 'youngest descendants' like the play?" said Simon.

"Yes," said Mr Dillon. "All of it was based on his plays."

"So how did Sally end up here? No disrespect, Sally," I said. I was still confused.

"Well, yes – that was a bit odd, but we were looking for the youngest daughter of Daphne when we found Sally and we made the video about her and collected all her details because we didn't know whether we'd find Julie. When we did track down Julie, we thought we might as well show Reginald both videos. He thought Sally resembled Daphne and was generally more appropriate for the inheritance than Julie, so he came up with the plan for voting off.

"That voting off idea comes from one of his plays – a play that was written way before *X-Factor* or *Big Brother* or any of those other voting off shows. This whole final act that he wrote was the summary of all of his plays."

"The plays he suddenly decided to take ownership of in death…" said Simon. "What a beautiful literary flourish."

"There was no way anyone was ever going to work out how we knew him, though," said Sally. "Why did he ask us to spend so long thinking about it, and deliver the clues like he did?"

"Just like he said - he wanted you to know the whole story and really think about how much impact your relatives had. He also wanted you to meet one another and spend time together."

"Do you think you'll find Tom Gower?" I asked. It was bothering me quite a lot that the detectives hadn't managed to do this yet.

"Yes. I'm confident we'll find him."

"Good," I said. "Just one final question – was it his idea to get one of us to do a speech? That was plain cruel."

"Yes," he said. "That little twist made him laugh a lot."

"I wish I could have met him," I said. "It's a shame we never got to."

"Read the plays," said Mr Dillon. "I think he poured every part of himself into the plays. You'll get to know who he was and what he stood for if you read them."

I nodded. I planned to read them all and learn as much about him as I could. I figured that the more I learned about him, the more I would understand the odd couple of days I'd just endured.

Once we'd finished questioning Paul, he bid us all farewell and Huw thanked him. We put ourselves into a WhatsApp group called 'Friends of Reginald' and promised to meet up on the anniversary of Reginald's death every year. We all hugged and swore that we'd keep in touch.

Chapter 32

I LEAPED ONTO THE TRAIN WITH ABOUT THREE SECONDS TO spare after a very embarrassing run down the platform, shrieking at the driver to wait as I dragged my huge case behind me. By the time I fell onto the train I could hardly breathe. I removed my coat and threw it over my arm before I went hunting for my seat.

The train was packed and there was no first-class carriage, so the solicitors' firm had booked me a seat in carriage F. I seemed to have joined the train in carriage D, so as the train moved off, making every step perilously difficult, I stumbled and staggered through the train like a drunk, heading for carriage F, seat 12A. The task of dragging a huge case full of clothes that I didn't wear behind me was proving hellishly difficult as I weaved through, trying to avoid feet, elbows and handbags. In my spare hand I carried my coat and a healthy supply of snacks.

There it was – seat 12A. The only problem was that someone else was sitting in it.

"Excuse me," I said. "I'm really sorry, but you're in my seat."

"Am I?" said the guy. I felt a bit bad kicking him out – he had a nice spread in front of him – crisps and sandwiches and a big cup of coffee, but there was nowhere else to sit.

He gathered his things together, putting his work notes under one arm, the sandwich and crisps in his hand and the rubbish from the food in the other, then attempted to pick up his coffee. The train jolted and he slipped, spilling coffee all over his clothes and his papers.

He dropped the work and the coffee and attempted to try and clean his shirt with his hands, but his hands were full, so we all looked on in mounting sympathy as he went to throw the rubbish he was carrying into the bin and accidentally threw his sandwich and crisps away by mistake.

"Shit," he growled. His shirt was soaked, his notes were ruined and his food was in the bin.

"I'm so sorry," I kept saying as he walked away, covered in coffee.

It wasn't my fault – he was in the wrong seat – but I'm British so I felt hellishly guilty even though it was entirely his own fault for not reading his ticket properly.

I settled into the still-warm seat as my phone bleeped. I opened it and read the message, it was a note in the WhatsApp group from Mike.

"Been doing a lot of thinking since we left the solicitors," he said. "I think we should all try and help find the Gowers. They obviously meant so much to Reginald and his dad, and we meant so much to him…it would be nice, don't you think?"

"I'm in," I replied. "I'd love to help out."

I was dying to go back to Mike and ask whether he'd seen Julie since we kicked her out, but that didn't seem appropriate.

"I'm in if Simon's in!" replied Matt. "We need him to organise us."

"Of course I'm in," said Simon. "I think that's a great idea."

Then a message from Sally. "I'm in too."

"How's Julie?" replied Simon, asking the question on the tip of everyone's tongue.

"In a massive sulk, but she'll get over it. Her boyfriend is worth millions so she doesn't need the money, it might teach her to be kinder. Mary, I'm really sorry for the way she spoke to you."

"Don't worry," I said. "It's fine."

"So how are we going to organise this, then?" asked Mike.

"Let me have a think and I'll come back with a plan," replied Simon.

"Great, looking forward to seeing you all soon for our next adventure!" I replied, and tucked my phone and ticket back into my bag.

No sooner had I put everything away than the inspector appeared at the far end of the carriage and I pulled my ticket back out again. It was only at that moment I realised I should have been in carriage E. Fuck. I'd caused all that drama and all that spilled coffee and it wasn't even my seat. I looked at the guy, standing by the door, his shirt featuring an unattractive brown stain, and felt a wave of guilt. I hoped he wouldn't realise he'd been in the right seat all along when the inspector checked his ticket.

Oh well, if he did – I'd give him his seat back. I'd even offer to pay for his shirt to be cleaned. Hey – I could offer to buy him a new shirt. Buy 20 shirts!

I sat back and closed my eyes. Life was a wonderful, fragile thing and it could change at any minute – for better or worse:

just look at the guy with the coffee all over him. While things were good, I needed to learn to count my blessings. From now on I was determined to enjoy every precious moment of life. I would cherish my family and friends more and be grateful for all the lovely things I had…even my grotty flat…and my ugly work uniform that makes me look like Kermit…and my weird boss…and the hellish-sounding weight loss camp I was I booked into in two weeks' time. Or, maybe not the weight loss camp – just the other things.

Did you enjoy the book? PRETTY PLEASE leave me a review if you did. Reviews mean so much to authors…x

This is the UK link to leave a review: My Book

Thank you!!

Want to find out what happens next?

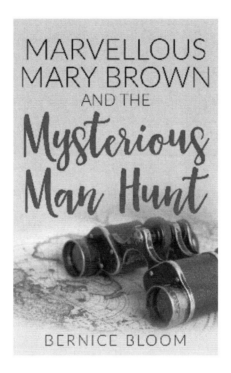

Marvellous Mary Brown and the Mysterious Manhunt is the follow-up to *Mysterious Invitation* in which we find out what happened to the Gower family and how they react when complete strangers bang on their door. OUT IN NOVEMBER 2020.

EMAIL:

bernicenovelist@gmail.com to join the newsletter list and be first to hear when the book is out…

AND IF YOU WANT TO FIND OUT WHAT HAPPENS WHEN MARY goes on the weight-loss camp, the book is on Amazon now

Also by Bernice Bloom

Just head to the the website to see all the books in the series:

www.bernicebloom.com

Or, join us on Facebook where we're laughing and having fun on:
www.facebook.com/bernicebloombooks

Twitter is: Bernice1Bloom

Thank you so much x

Published internationally by Gold Medals Media Ltd:

Bernice Bloom 2018

Terms and Conditions:

The purchaser of this book is subject to the condition that he/she shall in no way resell it, nor any part of it, nor make copies of it to distribute freely.

All Persons Fictitious Disclaimer:

This book is a work of fiction. Any similarity between the characters and situations within its pages and places or persons, living or dead, is unintentional and co-incidental.